Are you sure you want to turn these pages?
There's nowhere to breathe beyond this point.
And no way back once you start.

MOLOCH
The Real King of Horror

IAN BAYLY

A Dark Matter Story

ASHLAR
PRESS

FIRST EDITION

ISBN: 978-1-7642983-1-5

Published by Ashlar Press
www.AshlarPress.com
info@AshlarPress.com

Author Contact:
www.ianbayly.com
contact@ianbayly.com
Facebook & Instagram: @ianbayly.author
Patreon.com/ianbayly

Terrificus. - Latin
Meaning: Causing terror
"his body presented a terrific emblem of death"

Contents

Introduction

By Ian Bayly

You won't get to breathe.

That's not a warning, it's a design feature. The man at the centre of this story doesn't get a moment of peace, and neither will you. I didn't write this book for comfort. I wrote it to trap you. To put you inside the crawlspace where he lives, where every word tastes like ash and every shadow might speak. If you're still reading, you've already opened the door. The thing behind it is patient, but it's not kind.

Moloch is the second book in the Dark Matter mythos.

The mythos began with *Dark Matter: The Order of the Hidden Cross*, a metaphysical descent into fractured timelines, dimensional bleed, and esoteric truths buried beneath centuries of religious control. That book follows Joshua Carpenter—a child born with the ability to see what others cannot. From the moment of his birth, something has been whispering to him across dimensions. With the help of Beris, a strange and sometimes unreliable companion, Joshua learns to navigate these fractures. Not to conquer them, but to listen—to find the source of the whisper, and understand why it chose him.

Moloch is not a sequel.

There are no returning characters. No plotline to pick up where the last left off. You can read either book first—or alone—and it will still find you. But they are connected. Not through events, but through gravity. Through something older. Something with teeth.

Where Dark Matter explored the outer edges of forbidden knowledge, Moloch turns inward. This is the story of a writer. A man who wanted a quiet life. A steady one. But when a manuscript he never meant to share finds its way into the world—published without his consent—everything changes. The book is a hit. The voice returns. And the whisper becomes a demand.

Its name is Moloch.

His presence predates humanity. He is older than language, but wears many names. In some stories, he is a god of fire. In others, a machine. A principle. An instinct. In this one, he wears a smile. He feeds not only on children, but on what births them—love, sacrifice, dreams, art. Moloch is what happens when creation forgets why it began. He appears in thresholds. In bargains. In the silence between inspiration and decay.

The writer spirals. His success feeds him, but hollows him out. Each book comes faster. Less his. More automatic. He writes in trances. Wakes up to pages he doesn't remember crafting. Smiles he didn't mean. Words not his own. His wife, Martha, watches as he slips—not immediately, not all at once, but with the steady erosion of something being consumed from the inside. She has her own weight to carry. And eventually, her own line to cross.

Moloch is not a possession story in the usual sense. There are no spinning heads. No holy water. What occurs here is quieter, colder, and harder to name. It lives in ambition. In guilt. In the slow trade of truth for attention. The supernatural bleeds into the domestic, and what begins as whispers becomes intrusion— into dreams, into speech, into blood.

Like Dark Matter, this book contains artefacts. Fragments of newspaper clippings, annotated texts, found pages. These are not set dressing. They are evidence. If Dark Matter opened the kaleidoscope, Moloch twists it. The patterns shift. The symbols repeat. A name written in too many hands. A child speaking a line he could not know. These echoes are not accidents.

Both books exist inside a continuum. A mythos that expands not outward, but inward—through time, through grief, through cracks in the soul. There is no chosen one. No salvation. Just a growing awareness that what waits behind the veil is no longer waiting.

You do not need to read these books in order. But if you read them both, you'll begin to feel the shape of something moving beneath. Something that was always there.

This isn't fiction. Not exactly. It's a kind of a ritual. It's conjuring.

And if your hands are on this book—then you're already part of it.

'You think you're safe because you'll close the last page.
But I'm still here.
And *I'm* hungry again.'

"Every time you make a choice you are turning the central part of you, the part of you that chooses, into something a little different than it was before. And taking your life as a whole, with all your innumerable choices, all your life long you are slowly turning this central thing into a heavenly creature or a hellish creature: either into a creature that is in harmony with God, and with other creatures, and with itself, or else into one that is in a state of war and hatred with God, and with its fellow creatures, and with itself. To be the one kind of creature is heaven: that is, it is joy and peace and knowledge and power. To be the other means madness, horror, idiocy, rage, impotence, and eternal loneliness. Each of us at each moment is progressing to the one state of the other."

C.S. Lewis

Chapter 1

The Struggling Writer

Lately, everything read like a rejection letter, thin, impersonal, full of words that weren't for him.

The kitchen smelled of strong coffee and burnt toast, the warm aroma almost masking the lingering trace of yesterday's dinner, sausages, garlic, and tomato sauce, faintly sour. Morning light streamed in through the blinds, cutting the room into stripes of harsh white and soft shadow.

As he sat hunched at the table, his eyes locked on the oh too thin envelope resting under his fingertips. It was from Quill and Paper Publishing, and it carried the weight of a truth he had learned to anticipate: rejection.

Across the kitchen, Martha moved quickly, one eye on the kids and the other on the clock. She wore her favourite flannel robe, and her bare feet padded softly against the linoleum floor as she worked to keep Grace and Alex from breaking into a full-fledged argument over breakfast. Their shrill voices rose and fell like tiny waves crashing against a fragile dam, their energy too much for this early in the morning.

"Share, please," Martha said, her voice tight with forced calm as she slid a plate of toast halves in front of them.

The struggling writer sighed and fingered the edge of the envelope. He knew how this would play out; he could already feel the creeping heat of frustration gathering in his chest, like kindling before a flame.

He ripped open the envelope, his eyes scanning the page quickly.

Thank you for your recent submission. After careful consideration...

It was the same line as always, the one they all used. Rejection with a polite face, dressed in the same hollow words.

He crumpled the letter into a tight ball, the paper crunching under his grip like dry leaves, and he tossed it into the trash with a flick of his wrist, hoping to bury it along with his irritation.

For a second, his mind wandered, imagining the paper not in the trash but somewhere else, floating in flames, turning to ash like everything else he tried to create.

Martha's eyes flicked to the trash, then back to him.

"Another one?" she asked, careful not to press too hard.

He took a sip of his coffee. "Yeah," he muttered, the word dropping like a stone in his mouth.

Without hesitation, Martha walked over to the trash, bent down, and picked out the balled-up letter. The tension in her shoulders seemed to soften as she smoothed the paper flat, her fingers moving over each crease as if the act of straightening it could somehow take away the rejection's sting.

With a touch of sarcasm in her voice, she read aloud:

Dear Sir,

Thank you for your recent submission. After careful consideration, we regret to inform you that the world is simply not ready for what you have to offer. Your work delves into the supernatural horror genre in a manner that, while undeniably... unique, left us pondering whether the real horror is your narrative or the devil himself, punching in for a day at the office. Might we suggest a change of direction? Perhaps something a little more wholesome? A story with fewer demonic encounters and more of life's gentler moments might better capture your audience's hearts, and leave fewer of them clutching their crucifixes.

Kind regards,

Quill and Paper Publishing.

She shook her head and laughed, but her laugh had an edge, like trying to joke away a bad smell that wouldn't leave.

"That's just... ridiculous," she said, meeting his eyes with a soft smile. "It's funny, though. I'll give them that."

She walked over to the credenza just off the kitchen, opening a small wooden box with a heavy sigh. It was already mostly full, crammed with folded letters, some yellowing at the edges from age, others stark white and freshly read.

"Maybe we should bind these up, turn 'em into a book," she said, mouth twisted. *"Could call it Thanks, But No Thanks."*

He forced a smile but didn't respond, watching as she carefully slid the latest rejection in among its siblings. He didn't have the energy to argue, but the idea of those letters as a book felt too vivid. Maybe it was all he'd ever write, a collection of failures.

He imagined that book, a black cover, no title, and all those rejections printed back to back, mocking him page after page.

"You're really keeping all of them?"

"Of course," Martha said, closing the box and running a thumb over its grain. "One day, when you're rich and famous, you'll want to look back on these and laugh."

The kids' bickering grew louder, breaking the fragile calm in the room. Alex had snatched the last slice of toast, and Grace was tugging at it like a dog gnawing at a bone.

"It's mine!" she whined, high-pitched and piercing.

The struggling writer winced, feeling the noise grate against his already frayed nerves. He grabbed his coffee, muttered, "I'll be in my office," and walked away before the argument escalated further.

His "office" was a cramped little nook off the kitchen, really just a corner of the room where he'd jammed a tiny desk and a battered typewriter. Piles of paper sat in precarious stacks, some covered in notes, others marked with red ink, the ruins of stories that had never made it past their first drafts.

He sat down, his chair creaking under his weight. The typewriter stared back at him, blank and expectant. He took a deep breath and began to type.

"The baby's first cry split the night like a war horn..."

He stopped. The sentence looked all wrong, awkward and stiff, like a stranger wearing his clothes.

He yanked the page out of the typewriter, crumpled it in his fist, and tossed it across the room. He's good at that.

The paper hit the wall and bounced onto a growing pile of failures.

For a moment, he thought about the edge of his desk, how sharp it was, how it might feel pressed against his head if he fell onto it.

He shook his head, trying to dislodge the thought.

It wasn't the first time something like that had crossed his mind, and he hated that the dark seemed to circle back to that same place when he felt like this, like a bruise he couldn't help but press.

He couldn't do this. Not today.

Standing up, he grabbed his coat, walked back into the kitchen, and kissed Martha on the cheek.

"I'm going to work early."

She paused, looking at him with eyes that tried to be encouraging but carried a shadow of concern.

"All right, dear. Have a good day," she said, brushing a hand over his shoulder. "And remember, one day, they'll be calling you for interviews."

He snorted, more to himself than to her. "Yeah. One day."

The day moved with a dull throb, like a slow drumbeat he couldn't escape.

He taught English at the local high school, and by the afternoon, fatigue had settled into his bones.

In his last period, some of his students started whispering and snickering in the back row.

One of them, Kyle, a smirking teenager with too much confidence and not enough tact, waved a newspaper in the air, his voice cutting through the background noise with an edge that made the writer's stomach twist before the words even came.

"Hey, Teacher! We read your story in *The Gazette*. So, uh, do they pay you for that stuff, or do you just do it for fun?"

Laughter erupted around the classroom, bouncing off the

walls like an unwelcome echo, each chuckle tightening the knot in his chest. He clenched his jaw, forcing himself to relax, to play it cool, to remind himself that these were just kids, kids who didn't know the weight their words carried, kids who would go home and forget about this moment while it would carve itself into his ribs and settle there.

With an air of tired apathy, he looked at them and quirked a faint smile, the kind meant to deflect, to make it all seem like it didn't matter.

"Glad to know my work is being read," he said dryly, hoping the comment would glide over them, that they would let it drop, that he wouldn't have to sit in this discomfort any longer. "Now, how about we get back to *Hamlet*, yeah?"

The bell finally rang, a sound that should have felt like relief but instead felt like the inevitable breaking of a dam. Chairs scraped against the linoleum as students bolted from their seats, racing toward the door, toward their cars, toward the world outside that had never felt as claustrophobic to them as it did to him.

He gathered his papers slowly, methodically, feeling each second stretch and weigh down on him, the remnants of laughter still echoing in his skull.

Outside, his old '56 Plymouth sat waiting, a loyal but battered thing that had seen better days, much like its owner. He sank into the seat, the worn leather sighing beneath him, and turned the key in the ignition.

The car coughed, whined, and then went silent. He cursed under his breath, pumping the gas pedal, trying again.

This time, the engine sputtered to life, and he threw the car into reverse, backing out of his *Teachers Only* spot before it could change its mind.

He drove aimlessly at first, the roads blurring together as he tried to shake off the day's heaviness, but Martha's voice chimed in his head as he remembered.

"Don't forget the wine for tonight. And don't buy the cheapest one, okay? We might be broke, but we're not poor."

"Right. Mid-tier," he muttered to himself, scanning the street for a liquor store.

The sign for Dunworth's General Store came into view, the faded lettering barely visible against the overcast sky.

Pulling into the little strip mall parking lot, he barely registered the red and white 1958 Plymouth Fury until it was too late, jerking the wheel at the last second to avoid clipping it, his tires scraping against the curb.

He sat there for a moment, gripping the steering wheel, exhaling sharply. He'd never seen anything like it. It looked custom, one of a kind, pristine in a way that didn't belong in a place like this.

"Made in 'Merica," he muttered with a grin, shaking his head before stepping out of the car.

Inside, the store was cramped, dimly lit, the shelves overflowing with bottles of all shapes and sizes.

His eyes skimmed the price tags, his hand hovering over a ten-dollar bottle before Martha's voice echoed again in his mind, a quiet reminder of standards, of dignity, of not settling for less even when life tried to force it upon them.

He picked something better, a $29.99 cabernet, not fancy, but decent enough, just enough to keep up the illusion of choice.

Why not just call it thirty bucks, he thought as he made his way to the counter.

The Plymouth's owner was there, easy to spot in his red jacket, the car's name Fury emblazoned across the back in chrome script, a perfect match to the machine parked outside.

The pride radiated off him, something tangible, something bordering on obsession.

"Nice car, man," the struggling writer said, offering an acknowledging nod.

The man grinned, teeth flashing in a way that felt too sharp, too knowing.

"Yeah, but she can be a little temperamental, a bit like a jealous girlfriend when you spot a 'younger model.' Ha ha, you know what I mean?"

The writer nodded again, a polite smile, the kind you give when you don't want to invite more conversation.

He paid for the wine, watching as the man strutted out of the store, his movements almost too aggressive, something simmering beneath the surface, a quiet rage wrapped in a well-polished grin.

By the time he got home, the sky had turned soft indigo, the world slipping into that in-between space where daylight gave up and the night took over.

The stars were scattered across the sky like glitter against a velvet canvas, indifferent to the weight pressing down on him.

Martha was already at the door, waving at him with a smile that was tired but real, the kind of smile that made the whole day feel just a little less unbearable.

She didn't care if he brought back a cheap bottle or the most expensive vintage on the shelf, she just wanted him home, wanted them to feel normal for a little while.

He stepped inside, letting the warmth of the trailer settle around him, familiar and yet stifling all at once.

He set the bottle of wine on the counter, gave Martha a quick kiss, their lips barely brushing, an absent kind of affection, the kind that came from too many days spent carrying too many things alone.

"How was your day?" she asked, searching his face for something she could fix with an encouraging word, a small gesture, anything to soften the edges.

"Eh," he replied, shrugging as he took off his coat. "The kids read my story in the paper... they, well, they made fun of it."

Martha's smile faltered for half a second, just enough for him to notice, before she forced something reassuring into place.

"I'm sorry," she said softly, reaching out to touch his arm. "Kids can be cruel. But... look, at least they're reading. They're talking about your work, even if they don't understand it."

He nodded, but it felt hollow. They weren't talking about his work, they were laughing at it, at him. It wasn't discussion, it wasn't interest, it was a joke at his expense, and the worst part was that he knew it wouldn't be the last time.

As the night moved on, the feeling didn't leave him. It clung to his skin, to his thoughts, a weight he couldn't shake.

He stepped outside, taking a beer with him, letting the cool air bite at his skin. The street was quiet, nothing but the distant hum of a television leaking from a neighbour's window and the occasional rumble of a passing car.

And then he saw it.

The red and white Plymouth Fury.

Parked across the street, half-hidden beneath the dull glow of a streetlamp, its chrome glinting under the moonlight like a predator waiting in the dark.

His stomach twisted.

The guy from the liquor store didn't live around here. He was sure of it. And yet, there it was, sitting there like it belonged, like it had been waiting for him.

Coincidence. Had to be.

But the unease sat heavy in his chest as he turned back toward the door.

He stole one last glance over his shoulder.

The car was gone.

His breath caught.

Hadn't heard it start.

He wasn't sure he believed it was just a coincidence.

Forcing a smile as he stepped back inside, pushing the door shut with a quiet click, trying to shake the sensation creeping along the back of his neck.

Martha looked up from where she was sitting at the table, her eyes catching his just long enough to register something beneath the surface, a flicker of unspoken concern.

"Everything okay?" she asked, her voice gentle but measured, the way someone speaks when they already know the answer.

"Yeah. Just needed some air."

She didn't push, just shifted slightly, making room for him at the table, an invitation that felt heavier than it should have.

He sat down, the scrape of the chair against the floor louder than necessary, filling the space between them.

The wine sat unopened, the bottle dark and waiting. He thought about pouring himself a glass, thought about the slow burn of alcohol as it slid down his throat, thought about how it used to dull the edges that had started cutting deeper in the past few months.

Instead, he just stared at it.

The kids had long since gone to bed, their voices nothing more than a muffled backdrop of sleep-heavy murmurs behind closed doors.

The house felt settled, but he didn't.

Something about the way the night folded around the trailer, thick and unshaken, felt unnatural.

He tried to focus on Martha's voice, the casual rhythm of her words as she recounted her day, the small victories and frustrations wrapped up in grocery store encounters and neighbourly gossip.

He wanted to listen, wanted to let her words ground him in the normalcy of their life, but his mind kept drifting back to the street outside.

It wasn't just the car. It was the way it had disappeared.

He hadn't heard the engine. Hadn't seen the headlights flicker against the pavement. One second it had been there, and then it hadn't.

A coincidence.

It had to be.

He forced himself to focus, nodding in the right places, offering small hums of acknowledgment as Martha talked, but the weight in his chest wouldn't ease.

He wasn't even sure what he was afraid of.

The car? The man who owned it?

The way it made him feel like something was pressing just beneath the surface of reality, waiting for the right moment to make itself known?

"You're distracted," Martha said suddenly, breaking through the fog of his thoughts.

He blinked, shifting in his seat. "No, I, "

"You are," she interrupted, but her voice was soft, not accusing, just knowing.

She reached across the table, her fingers brushing against his. "Talk to me."

He hesitated, considering telling her, considering laying out the strange unease curling around his ribs like something living.

But how could he explain it? I saw a car that shouldn't have been there, and then it was gone? It sounded ridiculous even in his own head.

So instead, he just shook his head and gave her a small, tired smile.

"It's nothing. Just... long day."

She studied him for a moment, her fingers lingering before she pulled away, accepting his answer but not believing it.

"Okay," she said finally, but her voice caught. "You'd tell me... if it was something real, yeah?"

He nodded, lying.

Later, after the shower and a quick change into something that at least passed for put together, they drove to the Coopers' house for the dinner party.

The Coopers lived in a house that looked like it had been plucked from a home improvement magazine, clean lines, polished hardwood floors, decorations that spoke of curated taste rather than personal warmth. Everything in its place, everything just so.

As they walked up to the door, Martha squeezed his hand, the pressure small but deliberate, a quiet reminder that they were supposed to be here, that they belonged in this space even if it didn't feel like it.

The party itself was predictable. The same faces, the same conversations, the same polite inquiries about work and life and kids, the same undercurrent of small-town gossip that filled the air like background music.

Martha slid into the rhythm effortlessly, her laugh easy, her words light, weaving between conversations like she had always been a part of them.

He, on the other hand, hovered at the edges, sipping his wine slowly, nodding at the right times, letting the conversations swirl around him without fully engaging.

It wasn't long before the inevitable question found him.

"So, I hear you're a writer?"

The man asking was older, his greying beard neatly trimmed, his suit casual but expensive. There was something in his eyes that suggested curiosity but not genuine interest, the kind of question asked for the sake of asking, to fill silence rather than seek an answer.

He forced a polite smile, the well-rehearsed one that never quite reached his eyes. "Yeah, something like that."

"What kind of stuff do you write?"

"Mostly horror. Dark fiction."

The man's eyebrows lifted slightly, his mouth twisting into something between amusement and mild discomfort.

"Horror, huh? Guess that's a tough sell. Not exactly mainstream, is it?"

"Nope," he agreed, taking another sip of wine, letting the conversation die on its own.

It didn't.

"Ever think about writing something a little more... I don't know, accessible? Ever thought about writing something your kids could read?"

He smiled again, this time sharper. "I'll consider it."

The man nodded as if he had offered some profound wisdom, then turned his attention to someone else, the conversation dismissed as easily as it had started.

He exhaled slowly, setting his glass down, feeling the weight settle deeper.

He found a quiet corner, watching as Martha navigated the room with ease, envying her ability to fit, to belong.

She caught his gaze across the room, offering him a sympathetic smile, a small lifeline in the noise of it all.

He tried to return it, but it felt strained, like the muscles in his face no longer knew how to hold warmth.

By the time they finally got home, Martha looked exhausted.

She let out a deep sigh as she kicked off her shoes, stretching her arms above her head.

"I'm beat," she said, her back cracking with the motion.

"Think I'll get ready for bed. You coming?"

"In a bit," he replied. "I might just... write for a little while."

She hesitated in the doorway, studying him again, that same quiet concern from earlier still lingering.

"Okay. But don't stay up too late, okay?"

"Promise," he said.

They both knew it was a promise he wouldn't keep.

The trailer was quiet once Martha disappeared down the hall, the stillness stretching long and thin, the kind of silence that felt deliberate, unnatural.

The hum of the old Westinghouse refrigerator filled the space, a low, steady noise that had always been there, had always been part of the trailer, but tonight it felt intrusive.

He wandered toward his desk, the typewriter waiting, the blank page staring back at him like a pestilent child demanding attention.

He sat down, fingers hovering over the keys, waiting for something to come.

But instead, all he heard was the scratching.

Soft at first, barely there, a faint, rhythmic scrape against wood, coming from behind the wall.

His breath hitched. He told himself it was nothing. Just the trailer settling, just his mind playing tricks on him after the weight of the day.

But then it came again, longer this time. Deliberate. Not the sporadic shifting of old foundations, not the wind slipping through unseen cracks.

Something was in there.

His fingers curled against the desk, his pulse picking up as he strained to listen, his body rigid with a tension he couldn't name.

The scratching stopped.

But the silence felt worse.

The scratching had stopped, but its absence was not a relief. If anything, the silence felt heavier now, stretched too thin, like an old rope fraying at the edges.

He sat motionless at his desk, his breath shallow, ears straining for any sign of movement behind the wall.

The hum of the old refrigerator filled the space again, grounding him for a moment, but the sound did nothing to ease the tension coiling in his chest.

The rational part of him knew what it wanted to believe, that it was nothing, that old houses creaked, that the trailer settled differently at night, that his mind was exhausted from the weight of rejection, from the students' laughter, from the quiet judgment at the dinner party.

But the deeper, quieter part of him, the one that had always been open to the unknown, the part that wrote the kind of stories people turned away from, whispered something else.

His fingers hovered over the typewriter keys again, but the words did not come.

He stared at the blank page.

It mocked him, at the pile of crumpled drafts littering the floor, and he thought, Maybe this is it. Maybe the words are done with me.

The thought settled like a stone in his stomach.

Writing had always been his escape, his way of clawing his way out of the darkness.

But if the words were gone, if they had abandoned him, what was left?

A sharp creak echoed through the trailer, breaking the thought before it could fully form.

His breath caught in his throat, fingers clenching against the edge of the desk.

The sound had not come from the wall. This time, it had come from the hallway.

He turned his head slowly, pulse hammering against his ribs.

The trailer was dark, the only light coming from the weak glow of his desk lamp.

The hallway stretched beyond it, empty, but something about the shadows felt wrong, too deep, too still.

The door to the bedroom was closed. Martha was asleep. The kids were asleep.

He swallowed hard, forcing himself to exhale. Just tired. Just imagining things.

He pushed himself away from the desk, the chair scraping loudly against the wooden floor. The sound made him wince.

It felt too loud, too intrusive, as if it had called attention to him, as if something had been waiting for him to move.

He hesitated for a moment longer, then stood, shaking off the weight of his thoughts, forcing his legs to carry him toward the bedroom.

The hallway bit at his bare feet, colder than it had any right to be.

He walked quickly, not daring to look into the dark corners, not letting his eyes linger on the shadows that seemed to shift just out of sight.

By the time he reached the bedroom door, his hands were trembling.

He told himself it was from exhaustion, from stress, from the endless failures piling up in his life.

But when he slipped into bed beside Martha, pulling the covers over himself, he couldn't shake the feeling that something had been watching him the entire way.

Sleep did not come easily.

When he woke, it was still dark.

The clock on the nightstand read 3:16 AM, the kind of time that sat between real and unreal, the dead space of the night where things moved in the dark, where thoughts turned inward, where the mind whispered things it shouldn't.

The room was still, Martha's slow, even breathing the only sound.

For a moment, he thought he had imagined whatever had pulled him from sleep.

Then he heard it.

The scratching.

It was louder now.

Closer.

His stomach twisted as he turned his head toward the sound, his eyes adjusting to the dim light filtering in through the curtains. The noise wasn't coming from the walls this time. It was coming from inside the room.

His breath caught, and he went completely still, listening. The sound was deliberate, a slow, dragging scrape against wood, like fingernails skimming the surface of the nightstand. His nightstand.

His body felt disconnected from his mind, locked in place by something primal. Every instinct screamed at him not to look, not to acknowledge it, to stay still, to pretend he hadn't heard it. But his eyes betrayed him, flicking toward the source of the sound before he could stop himself.

Nothing.

The nightstand was empty.

But the sound was still there.

His breath was coming too fast now, his chest rising and falling in short, shallow bursts. He clenched his hands into fists beneath the covers, forcing himself to slow down, to think. The shadows in the room seemed thicker, the corners darker.

He turned his gaze toward the doorway, toward the hall beyond, and a fresh wave of unease crawled down his spine.

The door was open.

He was certain he had closed it before bed.

A single, cold bead of sweat rolled down his temple as he stared at the empty space beyond the threshold. The hallway was silent, stretching into the darkness, the weak glow of the kitchen light barely reaching past the doorway.

His ears strained for any sound, any shift, but there was nothing. The scratching had stopped. The house was silent again.

But the silence no longer felt empty.

It felt waiting.

Martha stirred beside him, shifting in her sleep, murmuring something unintelligible before rolling onto her side. The small, human sound grounded him, pulling him back from the edge of the fear coiling around his ribs.

He forced himself to take a slow, deep breath, then another. When he looked back toward the hallway, the open door, the stretching dark, he told himself he had simply forgotten to close it. That the sound had been nothing. That his mind was playing tricks on him, twisting exhaustion into something more sinister.

He closed his eyes.

Eventually, sleep found him.

By morning, the night before felt distant, like something half-remembered from a fever dream, still unsettling, but easier to dismiss under the weight of daylight. The sun streamed weakly through the curtains, turning the dust in the air to floating gold specks. The muffled sounds of Martha moving around the kitchen, the clinking of mugs, the soft muttering of the radio, grounded him back into reality.

He sat up slowly, rubbing a hand over his face, trying to shake the lingering tension coiled in his chest. His head ached, his body sluggish, as if he'd spent the night wrestling something unseen.

For a moment, he just sat there, staring at the floor, at the way the morning light stretched across the carpet. He had work in a few hours. More students to teach. More polite smiles that barely covered the condescension. More whispers that felt like tiny, deliberate cuts.

Instead of getting up, he sat at his desk, resting his fingers on the keys of his typewriter, the cool metal grounding him. The blank page waited, expectant, but he hesitated, staring at the empty space where words should be.

He exhaled slowly, tapping one key. Then another.

The first line came, simple and unobtrusive.

"The baby's first cry split the night."

He stopped.

Something about it felt... wrong. Not the words themselves, but the way they settled on the page. The way they sat there, waiting. His skin prickled, a slow, crawling sensation running along his arms.

He stared at the sentence, willing himself to find the problem, but there was none.

Still, he couldn't shake the feeling that it hadn't come from him.

His fingers hovered over the keys, the weight of something unspoken pressing down on him.

The smell of coffee drifted in from the kitchen. Martha's voice, faint, talking to the kids. The scrape of a chair.

The normalcy of it all should have comforted him. But instead, it only made the unease worse.

The typewriter sat silent, the sentence unmoving.

He swallowed and ripped the page from the machine. Crumpled it. Tossed it aside.

Not today.

Pushing away from the desk, he stood and stretched, rolling the stiffness from his shoulders. The weight in his chest hadn't lifted, but at least now, in the daylight, it felt manageable.

"Breakfast?" Martha called from the kitchen.

He ran a hand through his hair, forcing a small, tired smile before heading toward the smell of coffee and something almost like peace.

But as he left the room, a soft click echoed behind him.

The typewriter clicked. One key, slow and deliberate.

A single letter inked itself on the blank page.

Chapter 2

What Happens at the Cabin, Stays at the Cabin

The phone rang sharply, its mechanical chime cutting through the quiet of the small house. Martha wiped her hands on her apron, glancing towards the avocado-green rotary phone mounted on the kitchen wall. She sighed, picking up the receiver and curling the cord around her fingers as she brought it to her ear. "Hello?" "Martha, hi! It's Lena. Hope I'm not catching you at a bad time." Martha shifted, tucking the receiver under her chin as she leaned against the counter. "Not at all, Lena. What's going on?" "Listen, the boys are planning a trip up to the cabin this weekend. Just a couple of nights in the woods, campfires, fishing, drinking. You know how they are. I was wondering if you think he'd like to go?"

Martha let out a slow breath, glancing towards the nook just off the kitchen where he sat hunched over his typewriter. The small desk was crammed against the wall, covered in half-finished pages, crumpled rejection letters, and an overflowing ashtray. He wasn't writing, just staring, the keys untouched, a cigarette burning low between his fingers. Lately, his bad moods stretched longer, his frustration thicker. The latest rejection letter had hit him a little harder than usual, she thought.

"I don't know, Lena. He's been in a mood. Spends all day in that chair, barely looks up except to light another cigarette." "That's exactly why he should go," Lena pressed, her voice confident but kind. "Come on, it's just a couple of nights. Fresh air, good company. He needs this. And honestly, you probably need a break from him too." Martha exhaled, rubbing her forehead. She knew how this conversation would go. He'd refuse at first, say he had too much work to do, that he was close to a breakthrough, even though she knew he was just staring at a blank page half the time. But maybe, just maybe, if she framed it right... "All right," she said finally, tapping her nails against the countertop. "I'll talk to him. No promises, but I'll try." "Perfect! Let me know how it goes. The guys are leaving Friday afternoon. Ok, they can pick him up at four."

As the call ended, Martha hung up the receiver with a soft click and stared at it for a long moment. The kitchen smelled of coffee and cigarette smoke, the late afternoon sun casting long shadows across the chequered linoleum floor. A part of her wanted to believe that a weekend away with the boys would shake him loose from whatever had a hold on him. Another part of her knew better. She took a breath, squared her shoulders, and turned towards the laundry.

That evening, after dinner, Martha found him still in the same spot, the glow of the desk lamp casting sharp shadows against the nicotine-stained wallpaper. He was hunched over his typewriter, though she doubted he'd written a single word. A cigarette smouldered in the ashtray beside him, the smoke curling towards the ceiling in lazy spirals. Martha had already made up her mind before she even spoke the words. He could tell by the way she lingered near the table after dinner, washing the same plate three times, drying her hands on a dish towel long after they were dry. The way she finally turned toward him, pressing her lips together as if choosing her words carefully. "The boys are going to the cabin this weekend." She leaned against the counter, casual, but her eyes watched him closely. "Lena called. The boys thought it might be good for you to go."

He exhaled slowly, rubbing at the dull ache in his temple. Not this. Not now. He didn't have the energy to argue, but he also didn't want to go. 'I don't know, Martha.' He gestured vaguely toward the typewriter in the corner of the living room, where a half-smoked cigarette sat cold in the ashtray, another wasted night of blank pages. 'I have work to do.'

She crossed her arms. 'You've been sitting in that chair for weeks. Maybe stepping away from it for a couple of nights wouldn't be the worst idea.'

She didn't get it. Stepping away wasn't the problem. The problem was that every time he sat back down, the words still didn't come.

'I'm close to something,' he lied, running a hand through his hair.

She tilted her head, considering him. 'Are you?'

He clenched his jaw, fingers tightening around the coffee mug in front of him. He hated when she did this. Hated how she could see the cracks before he even admitted they were there.

'You could do with the chance to just let go and do nothing for a change,' she continued, her tone softer now. 'Step away from the desk for a bit. Clear your head.'

'Is that what you think I need?' he muttered. 'A bunch of guys getting hammered in the woods?'

'I think you need something,' she said simply.

He stared at her, wanting to push back, wanting to tell her she was wrong, but wasn't she? The writing wasn't working. The trailer felt too small. The silence had started whispering.

He swallowed, looking past her toward the window. The blinds were open just enough to see the street outside, washed in dim yellow from the streetlamp. His stomach twisted. The Plymouth Fury was parked at the end of the road. His breath hitched. The same red and white car from Dunworth's General Store. He blinked, willing his eyes to adjust, to tell him he was wrong. But no, it was there. Sitting. Waiting. Martha hadn't noticed. She was still watching him, waiting for an answer. He tore his gaze away from the window. "Fine," he muttered, pushing back from the table. "I'll go." She let out a breath, relieved. "Good." When she turned away, he looked back at the window. The car was gone. The unease sat heavy in his chest.

The drive out to the cabin stretched longer than it should have, each mile folding in on itself like a road that never truly ended. The struggling writer sat wedged in the back seat, packed between coolers of beer and crumpled bags of crisps, the smell of stale snacks and sweat thick in the cramped car. His old college friends, Matt, James, and Colin, bantered like boys on a joyride, their voices bouncing through the vehicle, filling every inch of empty space. At first, he'd been reluctant to go. He told Martha it wasn't a good time, that he had work to do, but she had just smiled in that soft, knowing way of hers. "You could do with the chance to just let go and do nothing for a change," she'd said, brushing a hand over his arm. "Step away from the desk for a bit. Clear your head." He wasn't sure if she had meant it, or if she just wanted him out of the house.

Outside, the road twisted through the dense forest, a narrow stretch of faded asphalt winding between towering firs. The trees loomed taller as they drove further, their thick, tangled branches blotting out the last light of day. The further they went, the more the world seemed to shrink, the small town and all its obligations dissolving into the dark void of the wilderness. When they finally pulled up to the cabin after three solid hours of driving north, the sun was sinking fast, bleeding into the sky in deep, unnatural shades of orange and purple. The colours were saturated, sharp, like an image on an old television with the saturation turned up too high.

The forest air was heavy with Balsam Fir, Red Maple, Red Spruce, American Beech, Paper Birch, and Northern White-Cedar, damp earth mixing into a scent thick with decay. But beneath it lurked something else, like the smell of rain before a storm. For just a moment, as he stepped out of the car, he swore he saw the trees shift, not swaying with the wind, but bending, moving of their own accord, as if something unseen was slipping between them. He shook the thought away, too tired and annoyed to be there to think anything more of it.

As expected, the first night passed in a blur of beer and belly laughs, the kind of drunken nostalgia that only men who refuse to grow up can summon. They sat by the fire, tossing back cans and recounting stories of high school fights, college flings, the mysterious hot chick that got away 'that no one else met, and exaggerated victories. But as the night deepened, and the beer loosened their tongues, the conversation inevitably turned to him. Him sitting there getting drunk but not engaging in the conversation as intended.

Matt leaned in, arm slung over his shoulders, breath thick with alcohol and the sweet smell of a cigar. "So, how's the writing going, man?" The struggling writer stiffened even more, uncomfortable with being touched. Hugged. "Any bites from publishers?" Colin added, taking a slow drag from his cigarette. "When's that big book gonna be done?" someone asked. He forced a smile, let out a hollow laugh. "It's getting there." But they weren't satisfied. They wanted to know more. What the struggling writer didn't know was that this whole weekend was an intervention of sorts, conspired by everyone but him. "Maybe you need to loosen up, dude," Ray grinned, reclining against the nearby tree stump. The firelight cast flickering shadows over his face, making him look less human, more like a hollow thing wearing a man's skin. "You know, get those creative juices flowing."

James, who had been rolling a joint, smirked. "I know what he needs." Giggling at the thought, he pulled a tiny plastic bag from the pocket of his red and black plaid flannel. Inside, a handful of delicate squares, thin, translucent paper laced with fractal designs. "Ever done acid before, bud?" The struggling writer hesitated, heart beating a little too fast. Unsure what to do. "Nah," he muttered. "That's... not really my thing," he blurted out. "C'mon, man." Matt leaned in, his voice lower now, more coaxing. "Just one tab. It'll open your mind a little." The others chimed in, their voices rising, merging into a single, insistent chant. Do it, do it, do it. A wind stirred through the trees. The branches groaned like stretching bones. The fire burned bright, erratic. The shadows around them twisted, reaching toward the struggling writer as if urging him forward.

And then... he heard it. A whisper, slithering through the air. Not from his friends. Not from the fire. Something else. Do it. A deeper, more primal enticement. This was stupid, he thought to himself. But what if they were right? What if this was exactly what he needed? A way to break free, to loosen the grip of the constant rejection, the constant self-doubt. "Fine," he said as he snatched the tab from James's fingers. Immediately, without hesitation or opportunity to back out, he placed it under his tongue. It dissolved instantly, leaving behind a bitterness that coated his throat like ash, causing him to contort his face in discomfort. He swallowed hard, but the stubborn lump wouldn't budge. His palms felt clammy, his pulse loud in his ears.

At first, it was nothing. Just a slight buzz, a looseness in his limbs. The edges of the world softened, as if reality had been lightly sanded down. Then, the fire began to move. Not flickering, not dancing, moving. The flames coiled inward, like hands grasping at something unseen, their movements synchronized, as if they had become sentient. The smoke rose in patterns, forming faces, words, spirals that lingered for a moment before dissolving into the night sky above. The stars pulsed, their light warping, bleeding into streaks that smeared across the sky. The laughter of his friends became distorted, stretching and warping, melting into high-pitched wails and guttural howls. He blinked.

His hands, they weren't right. Too long, too stretched, the skin shifting beneath his touch like melting wax. He rubbed his fingers together, but they felt wrong, as if the sensation was delayed, out of sync with reality. And then… a new sound. Louder than the others. Not human. Laughter. But not from his friends. At the edge of the firelight, a figure stood, watching. Tall. Unnaturally tall. Its form was made of darkness, but it wasn't just a shadow, it had weight, presence.

And its eyes. Not empty. Devouring. Two voids pulling in the firelight, the world itself seeming to bend toward them. Inside those voids, tiny embers glowed, pulsing like something alive, something ancient. A name surfaced in the struggling writer's mind. Moloch. The figure grinned. "You've come so far," it purred, voice like silk wrapping around his throat. The struggling writer wanted to look away, but he couldn't. "And yet, every page you write feels like a betrayal, doesn't it?" The words slipped into his skull, threading through his thoughts like a parasite burrowing deep.

"Every story, a failure." "Every sentence, a disappointment." "Every word, a wound that never heals." He tried to move, but his limbs felt heavy, weighted down by something unseen. Moloch stepped closer, his form folding in on itself, shrinking into something human, but not quite. His limbs bent unnaturally as he became man-sized, his smile too wide, his eyes still too deep. "Let me help you." And suddenly, the fire was gone, replaced by mirrors. A thousand reflections. Each one a different version of him.

One stood on a stage, holding a book before a roaring crowd. One sat alone in a dark room, buried under unfinished manuscripts. One watched as Martha walked away, her back turning from him for the last time as she left with another man. Moloch's voice dripped into his ear, smooth and slow. "I can give you everything. Success. Recognition. Immortality." But then, he hesitated. His mind clung to the last fragment of doubt. A whisper of Martha's voice, Come back to me.

Moloch's grin widened, his voice soft, persuasive. "You get to choose, my friend. Your future is in your hands." The world pulsed. Then the mirrors shattered. And as the shards sliced through the air, the struggling writer felt himself lean forward. Felt his lips begin to form a word. "Yes, " "Dude, you okay?" Matt's voice. Too loud. Too real. The struggling writer snapped his mouth shut, vision blurring. He barely processed Matt's hand on his shoulder, the distant sound of laughter, the fire's crackle. He felt himself grounded back into the world for just a second, just long enough for his friend's voice to tether him.

His breath shuddered out. "Yeah." But he wasn't speaking to Matt. Moloch grinned. "Yes. I knew you would." At that moment, the hallucinations didn't fade. Reality did.

The world was still spinning when he woke. His body felt leaden, his mouth thick with the rancid aftertaste of alcohol and acid, as though he had been chewing on pennies in his sleep. The early morning chill clung to his skin, seeping through the fabric of his clothes, what was left of them. A groggy blink brought the scene into focus. The remnants of last night's fire smouldered, wisps of smoke curling into the air. The struggling writer lay sprawled in the dirt, his head resting against a log. His shirt was half-unbuttoned, his jeans undone, and, he realised with a mounting sense of dread, his boots were on the wrong feet.

Laughter crackled from the cabin's front steps. "Jesus Christ, you look like you had one hell of a night," Matt called, nursing a steaming mug of coffee, a devilish grin spread across his face. The struggling writer pushed himself upright, his body protesting every movement. Something felt off. His back ached like this for the first time, protesting that he's not as young as he used to be. James ambled over and handed him a dented tin mug. "Coffee? You're gonna need it." "Why do I feel…" He swallowed against the nausea, pressing his palm to his forehead. "Why do I feel like I got hit by a fucking train?"

"Well," James smirked, "maybe because you were dancing naked by the fire." The struggling writer stopped mid-sip. "Yeah," Ray chimed in, stifling a laugh. "Not just dancing, either. You performed for us, man. It was magical. We got, like, front-row seats to the most erotic, deeply unsettling display of interpretive dance the world has ever seen." "You also thought beer was water," Colin added from the cabin steps, flicking his cigarette. "Kept chugging it and immediately throwing up. But that didn't stop you."

The struggling writer groaned, rubbing his temples. His head pounded with a mix of shame and residual intoxication. He was too afraid to look down, to check if they were lying about the naked part. "Oh, and, uh…" Matt coughed into his fist, barely containing his amusement. "You might wanna check your face." The struggling writer's stomach dropped. Slowly, he reached up, running his fingers over his forehead. Ink. He scrambled to his feet, nearly toppling over, and rushed inside to find a mirror. There, in thick, smudged black marker, was a crude masterpiece of dicks and profanities scrawled across his face.

He stormed back outside, met with the howling laughter of his friends. "You absolute cunts," he muttered, collapsing onto a log beside the firepit, accepting his fate. James clapped him on the back. "Hey, man, it's a rite of passage. You were a legend last night." The struggling writer took a long sip of coffee, sighing as the warmth settled in his chest. He should have been furious. But somehow, as much as his head ached, as much as the shame simmered in his gut, he couldn't help but feel… lighter.

Martha would kill him if she ever found out. But for now, he let himself chuckle along with them.

The day stretched on in an easy haze. After a breakfast of bacon and eggs, the best hangover cure, according to Mike, they took their fishing rods down to the lake. The ice was thick, but the sound of it groaning under their weight made the struggling writer uneasy. The wind howled through the trees, rattling bare branches, while the lake beneath them let out deep, resonant moans as though it were alive. They sat in folding lawn chairs, bundled in layers, lines cast out in the hopes of catching some salmon for supper.

It was peaceful, until it wasn't. None of them noticed Colin's chair slowly creeping across the ice, the movement so gradual it was almost imperceptible. Until, Crack. Thud. Splash. The moment hung in stunned silence before panic erupted. Colin was gone. "Shit! Shit!" Matt scrambled to his feet. The struggling writer's breath caught in his throat, his own limbs locked in terror. Colin's arms flailed beneath the ice, his body trapped under the thick sheet. His panicked face twisted in horror, bubbles escaping his lips.

"Get him out!" Ray shouted. The ice was too thick. They clawed at it, pounded with their fists, but it wouldn't break. Colin thrashed beneath them, his lips already turning blue. "Fucking move!" Matt sprinted towards the truck. Seconds dragged into eternity.

The struggling writer dropped to his knees at the edge of the broken ice, only as close as he could without falling in himself. Fingers becoming numb scrabbling at the surface as if he could claw Colin out with sheer will. His knuckles smashed against the frozen sheet, again and again, raw and useless. The ice wouldn't give. It mocked him, unyielding, like the blank page. Behind him, voices blurred. Someone screamed for the axe. He couldn't move. He couldn't breathe. All he could do was hammer at the ice until the skin split and blood bloomed across the ice. When Matt came sprinting past, he barely registered it, just kept hitting the ice, like if he stopped, it would mean something final.

Colin's movements slowed. His eyes rolled back. Then, A deafening crack rang out. Matt stood over the hole, axe in hand, panting. The blade had shattered through, jagged chunks of ice floating in the water. Ray and James lunged forward, plunging their arms into the freezing abyss and dragging Colin up and out. His body hit the ice, motionless, a sickly blue hue spreading over his skin.

'Do something!' James didn't hesitate. He tilted Colin's head back, pressing his mouth to his lips and forcing air into his lungs. One beat. Two. Three. Colin coughed violently, water spewing from his lips as he sucked in a desperate, ragged breath. Relief crashed over them. 'Jesus Christ,' Matt muttered, hauling Colin to his feet.

They moved fast, dragging him back to the cabin, stripping off his soaked clothes and bundling him in blankets by the fire.

The struggling writer didn't follow. Not right away.

He stood at the door, breath misting in the cold air, hands still trembling and bloodied. The others barked orders, worked in sync, saved a life.

And what had he done?

He stared at the smudges of red across his knuckles, the sting beginning to creep in now that the adrenaline had ebbed. His fists had beaten the ice to no effect. No cracks. No rescue. Just blood. Just noise.

The laughter from inside was distant. Muffled. He felt like a ghost.

Eventually, he stepped through the threshold, his presence barely noted. No one mentioned his hands. No one even looked at him.

So, he made tea.

Colin sat shivering, hands wrapped around a steaming mug. He exhaled slowly, staring into the flames. 'That… was a come to Jesus moment, boys.' Silence hung heavy. Then, unexpectedly, Colin let out a breathless laugh. 'Holy fuck. I actually saw a light. Thought I was meeting the big guy.' Ray smirked. 'What'd he say?' Colin shook his head, voice hoarse. 'Told me to go back, 'cause my wife would kill me if I died out here.'

Laughter broke the tension, rolling through the cabin like thunder.

The struggling writer, still gripping his untouched mug of tea, watched them from his chair by the fire. They had saved their friend's life today, and he had done nothing but boil water. He wasn't sure how he felt about that. They didn't fish on the lake again. They made an unspoken pact not to tell Colin's wife what had happened, not until he was warm, dry, and far away from the ice. Instead, they spent the evening around the fire, drinking slow and steady, letting the adrenaline settle. The struggling writer, feeling oddly lighter than he had in weeks, found himself telling ghost stories by firelight, spinning twisted tales until the shadows seemed to creep in closer.

For the first time in years, he felt something shift inside him, not just the high, not just the fear, but something darker. Something waiting. The drive home on Sunday was quiet, the kind of silence that settles between men who have lived through something together; the kind that doesn't need to be spoken about. Colin sat in the front passenger seat, wrapped in extra layers, still shaking off the chill of death. The others swapped stories, laughter breaking through now and then, but the highlight of the weekend, the thing they would retell again and again, was the struggling writer's acid trip.

'Funniest fucking thing I've ever seen,' James said, shaking his head. 'You… prancing around like some pagan god, covered in your own vomit.' 'I still can't believe he thought he was being chased by a fucking dragon,' Matt added. The struggling writer just grinned, staring out at the endless road ahead. The real hallucinations hadn't stopped. Even now, in the daylight, he swore he saw something in the trees, just beyond the bend of the road, a shape, watching, lurking just beyond his vision.

As they got back into town, the struggling writer was dropped off first. As the car pulled up to his place, he stepped out, slinging his bag over his shoulder. The others waited for a moment, appreciating his antics once more, before offering lazy waves as they peeled off towards their own homes. He stood there for a moment, staring at the small double wide trailer.

From the outside, it was the same as ever, just four metal walls, a door, and windows that barely let in any light, but after this weekend, it felt different. Like it held something unknown, something waiting to be observed.

Schrödinger's trailer, he mused with a smirk. Either it contained the same old story or something new. The only way to find out was to step inside. Choosing to embrace whatever was waiting, he walked up the steps and pushed open the door. The scent of home hit him immediately, faint coffee, a hint of soap, something cooking. Martha was at the sink, her back turned, casually drying a plate. He stepped in quietly, watching her for a moment: the familiar sight of her, the way she moved, the subtle hum she let slip when she thought no one was listening. He had missed her more than he realised.

Without a word, he stepped behind her, sliding his arms around her waist. She tensed for a brief second before relaxing against him, a soft sigh escaping her lips. 'You're back,' she murmured. 'Yeah.' His voice was lower than usual. He pressed a kiss to the side of her neck, inhaling the warm scent of her skin. 'Where are the kids?' 'Out playing.' 'Oh, good.' He pulled her closer, the warmth of her body melting against his. She felt it then, the hunger in his touch, something different, something raw. 'Oh God,' she whispered, half-teasing, half-breathless. 'What on earth has possessed you?' He only smirked, pressing against her, showing her exactly what he had in mind as he hitched up her dress.

Chapter 3

A Hunger That Can't be Fed

That night, something was off. During dinner, the thoughts came first, half-formed, intrusive, slipping into his mind like a parasite that had always been there, waiting. They were not his thoughts. They couldn't be. Blasphemous, obscene, violent things. Concepts he had never dared to entertain, words he had once thought profane. They coiled around the rigid framework of his upbringing, the remnants of Sunday sermons, the voice of his father telling him that there were lines a man should never cross. Yet here they were, slithering through the cracks in his mind, filling the void with new ideas, dark ideas. And he could not stop them.

He tried to push back, to regain control. To think of good things, wholesome things, things that belonged in the light. But it was like trying to hold onto sand with trembling fingers, the more he resisted, the faster it slipped through. He felt like a man standing at the edge of a precipice, looking down into an abyss that whispered his name, beckoning him to step forward. His body jerked suddenly, his breath hitching, fingers twitching involuntarily. His mind convulsed, glitching in and out of rationality, fragments of thought colliding like shattered glass. The Methodist teachings of his childhood screamed at him to stop, to cast out whatever was infiltrating his thoughts, to get on his knees and pray. But another voice, new, seductive, laughed at the absurdity of such notions.

What if they lied to you? What if the darkness was always where the truth lay?

His hands gripped his skull, pressing against his temples as though he could physically stop the onslaught. He squeezed his eyes shut, muttering under his breath. And then, click-clack.

He froze. His breath hitched. The sound of the typewriter key striking paper echoed through the trailer. But the machine was cold, untouched. He turned sharply, but there was nothing there. Just silence. His reflection wavered in the dim kitchen window, something slightly off about it, as though it was still watching him even when he turned away.

"Stop. Stop. STOP."

A warm touch landed on his shoulder. He flinched, looking up to see Martha standing over him, concern knitting her brow.

"You're shaking," she said softly. "And sweating. What's going on?"

He exhaled, trying to steady his breathing. "Nothing. Just… thinking."

Martha wasn't convinced. She moved behind him, resting her hands on his tense shoulders. Her thumbs pressed into the knots in his muscles, slowly working them loose.

"You're overworked. You never let yourself rest, always trying to force something out of that typewriter."

"I have to," he muttered.

"No, you don't."

He let out a bitter chuckle. "Then why do the words keep coming?"

She didn't have an answer. Instead, she kept kneading the tension from his back, her touch grounding him, pulling him away from the madness clawing at his mind.

"Just let go," she whispered. "Let it come out. Whatever it is."

And that night, something did come out. Sitting at his typewriter, unsure of how to proceed, he places his itching hands on the keys, his left index finger on the F and the right index finger on the J. Then, in a matter of moments, the words simply flowed like they never had before. At first, chaotic words were randomly thrown onto the page, then, as if his mind and fingers started to align, the words started to make sense. There was no hesitation, no frustration, just a feverish, unstoppable force driving his fingers over the keys.

He wasn't thinking anymore. He wasn't guiding the story. He was listening.

There were sounds, not from the room, but from just behind his ears. A low hum like vibrating glass, and underneath it, a voice. Not a voice he recognised, but one he understood.

Zih'roth ven'al mach shul...

The words made no sense, yet they pulled meaning from him. They weren't instructions, but confirmations. Approvals.

Yes, the voice said. That's it. Bleed it out. You know the shape of things.

He smelled sulphur. Then rust. Then the sharp, sickly-sweet scent of burnt hair. He winced but kept typing. The air around him felt heavier with each keystroke, as if the act of writing had become an invocation.

His fingers moved faster, the muscles in his hands cramping, but he didn't stop. Couldn't stop. The typewriter clattered on, louder than it should've been. Like bones tumbling down a metal chute.

And just beneath the rhythm of it all, he heard Moloch laugh.

The clatter of the typewriter filled the small nook off the kitchen, pages piling up beside him, each word spilling forth with an urgency that he didn't question. He didn't dare question it.

The story that started to emerge was unlike anything he had ever written, dark, raw, and alive in a way that unsettled him. It breathed. The sentences moved with a rhythm that felt foreign, as though they were dictated rather than created. But he didn't stop. He couldn't stop. The hunger to keep writing burned in his chest, something deeper than inspiration, something... unnatural.

Later, when he looked back on those pages, he wouldn't remember writing a single word.

Over the next few days, Martha noticed the change almost immediately. He barely slept, and when he did, it was restless, punctuated by murmured words and sudden jerks. He stared into nothing for long stretches of time, lost in thought, fingers twitching as though he was still at the typewriter even when he wasn't. There was a hunger in his eyes she'd never seen before, something feverish, something not entirely his own.

Then, after days of relentless writing, he crashed. His body, finally giving in to the exhaustion, collapsed into bed. Martha barely had time to cover him with a blanket before he was gone, slipping into a sleep so deep it unsettled her. A day passed. Then another. By the third day, she had to check his pulse, feeling a spike of fear that something was wrong.

By the fourth day, now Monday, she called the principal.

"He's got the flu," she lied. "He's in bed, can't even sit up."

By the fifth day, she called the doctor. He wasn't sick. He wasn't dehydrated. His pulse was steady, strong even. His breathing was perfect, his temperature normal.

He was simply… gone.

The doctor could only offer vague reassurances.

"It's exhaustion," he said. "Leave him be. If he doesn't wake by the end of the week, we'll have to look at hospitalisation."

They couldn't afford a hospital. They had no insurance. So, she waited. He was speaking in his sleep. But not English. Not even a language she recognised. Latin. Hebrew. A third, unrecognisable tongue that made her skin crawl. She couldn't tell, but it seemed like he was speaking, and through him, someone was answering back.

While he slept, Martha read his manuscript. From the very first page, something about it unnerved her. The prose was brilliant, terrifying, filled with imagery that made her skin prickle. It didn't read like his usual writing, it was something else entirely.

For years, she had watched him struggle, rejection after rejection eating away at him. Now, suddenly, he had produced something unlike anything she had ever seen. Where was this coming from?

But when she looked at his sleeping form, peaceful for the first time in years, she shook her head. He needed this. He deserved this. If this book got published, maybe they could finally move out of this damn trailer. Maybe their kids wouldn't have to grow up hearing the roof creak under the weight of storms.

Martha knew her husband's writing inside and out. She had been his editor, his proof-reader, his reluctant critic for years.

But this? This was different.

She turned the pages with growing unease, her fingers trembling slightly. It was brilliant, unlike anything he had ever written. But it was also deeply personal. And then, she reached it.

A paragraph. A secret.

Her breath hitched, and she scanned the words again, her heart hammering against her ribs. It wasn't about childhood, nor was it something buried in the past. This was something far worse. Something she had only ever thought about.

Her hands clenched the paper. The manuscript described an affair, a fantasy she had never spoken aloud, never acted on. The way she had imagined it, the stolen glances, the brush of a hand, the lingering tension, the heat of a moment just before it tips into something irreversible.

He knew.

Every detail, down to the precise way her skin flushed at the thought. The way she lay awake sometimes, staring at the ceiling, indulging the forbidden scenario until guilt forced her to roll over and push it away.

He even knew the name.

The name she had never uttered aloud.

Her mouth went dry. Martha raced back, flipping frantically through her own old journals, her breath coming in short gasps as she scanned page after page. Nothing. No mention of it. No trace. She pressed her knuckles against her temple, trying to mentally retrace her thoughts. Had she ever let it slip? In a dream? A drunken conversation?

No. Impossible.

It was hers alone. Buried in her mind, locked away where no one, not even him, should have been able to reach it. But it was here. On the page. Staring back at her in his handwriting.

Her pulse roared in her ears as she turned the page, expecting an answer. Expecting some logical explanation, a coincidence, anything. Instead, the next passage began describing something worse. Something that hadn't happened outside of her fantasies.

Her hands trembled as she read the next few lines. It wasn't a hypothetical anymore. It was real. A desire written in black ink. The affair wasn't just imagined in his story, it was inevitable.

And the worst part?

She wanted it. She dreamt it over and over again.

A cold, creeping sickness coiled in her stomach. She shut the manuscript, staring at it like a venomous thing. It wasn't just a story anymore. It was an invitation. A possibility made real.

Martha glanced towards the bedroom where he slept, his face still and peaceful, his lips slightly parted as he muttered something in that strange, impossible language. Her fingers tightened around the edges of the manuscript.

She wanted to wake him, to shake him, to demand answers, but what would she even ask? How could he know? And worse...

Did she want to find out?

Martha picked up the manuscript again, her fingers ghosting over the pages, the weight of them heavier than it should have been. As with all his submissions, she took it upon herself to edit and correct some of the work, careful, so careful, not to change anything. Not even that.

Her eyes flicked to those passages, the ones that had turned her stomach, made her skin prickle with something too close to shame. She told herself it didn't matter. That it was just a story. Just words.

Her stomach churned as she sat down at the typewriter, feeding in a fresh sheet of paper. The machine stared back at her, cold and waiting, the ink ribbon stiff, the keys eager beneath her fingers. She placed her hands on the keys and hesitated, her breath shallow.

She could stop. She should stop.

Instead, her fingers pressed down, and the clatter of the typewriter filled the silence.

The sound felt deafening in the quiet house, each keystroke hammering out her complicity. She retyped his words exactly as they were, not daring to alter a single thing. Not even the parts she wished she could erase. Not even that.

When she finished, she pulled the last page free, setting it on top of the growing stack beside her. The manuscript was thick, a towering thing, unwieldy and heavy as she gathered it all together. She smoothed the pages, aligning them carefully, her hands lingering on the cover sheet.

She sat there for a long moment, staring at it. She could just… leave it. Walk away. Let it sit there on the desk where it belonged. But she didn't.

Instead, she retrieved a large envelope from the small credenza. It was stiff and unforgiving, but she managed to slide the entire manuscript inside. The paper barely fit, forcing her to shake it gently to make sure it settled properly. She pressed down the metal clasp, sealing it shut.

Her fingers lingered over the agent's name and address, which she had written in slow, deliberate strokes. And then she froze. The pen hovered over the return address. Her pulse thudded in her ears.

She could still stop. Her hand twitched as she held the envelope against her chest, the weight of it pressing down on her ribs. She could set it aside. Tear it open. Burn it, even. No one would ever know.

Her grip tightened. She was imagining things. That was all.

Still, when she walked to the mailbox, she kept the envelope clutched tightly, her breath coming in shallow pulls. The latch on the box was cold beneath her fingers. She hesitated; the envelope poised over the slot.

If she mailed this, she couldn't take it back.

One second passed. Then two.

And then, before she could change her mind, she shoved the envelope inside, the clang of the metal door slamming shut echoing louder than it should have.

Martha stepped back quickly, as if the mailbox might reach out and take her, too. She stared at it for a long moment, then swallowed hard and turned away.

She wouldn't tell him. He would never do it himself. He would sit on it for months, terrified of rejection. So, she had done it for him.

She told herself she was doing the right thing.

She walked back to the house with brisk steps, trying not to look over her shoulder. Inside, everything was too quiet.

The kind of quiet that made you feel like you weren't alone, even when you were.

She sat at the kitchen table, fingers tapping the surface. The kettle had long since gone cold. She poured herself a cup anyway, hands trembling. It tasted like nothing.

The guilt didn't arrive in a rush, it seeped in. Slow. Measured. Like water rising behind a dam.

She shouldn't have done it. Not without asking. Not with how fragile he'd been. Not with what she'd read in those pages.

But she told herself it was for the best. He wouldn't have sent it. He would've let it rot on the desk like every other finished thing. And this wasn't just another story. This one... this one mattered.

Didn't it?

She stared out the kitchen window. For the first time in years, the typewriter was silent. And that silence, it didn't feel like peace.

It felt like a waiting room.

It didn't take long before *Night Sky Magazine* accepted it. Almost immediately, in fact, praising its unrelenting atmosphere and visceral originality. They titled it *The Glass Floor*. His first real success.

That morning, just before his eyes finally opened, the house felt weird. Not loud. Not broken. Just... wrong. Like something had taken a step back and was watching to see what happened next. He started to stir from the bed with what seemed like a hangover, but in reality, it was just dehydration and soreness from oversleeping. It was like he hadn't slept in years. Martha helped him to his feet and guided him to the bathroom.

"Have a shower, darlin'. I'll make you some soup and crusty bread."

His stomach growled at the mention of food. He hadn't eaten in a week. She had been sponging water into his mouth to keep him hydrated, just as the doctor had suggested.

Now sitting on the couch, vaguely remembering the past week, Martha had to fill in a few details for him. He knew he had been writing, but he had no idea he had passed out for so long.

"You slept like the dead," she said.

"I feel like I'm dead," he muttered.

It took a few more days of recovery before he finally returned to the classroom. This time, he was different.

His students noticed first. The man who once stumbled through lessons, who had let their whispers and jokes roll off his back, now commanded the room with a quiet, unsettling presence. The lessons were sharper, more engaging. The words that fell from his mouth were precise, cutting through their teenage dissent like a blade.

They listened with interest now, leaning forward, absorbing his every word. Even the troublemakers sat still, eyes locked on him as he spoke. Their writing improved. Their comprehension sharpened. Test scores went up. They didn't understand why, but something about him made them want to be better.

And at the back of the room, unseen by all, Moloch watched.

A week later, Martha found him in the kitchen, the envelope from *Night Sky Magazine* trembling in his grip. She reached for it, but he wouldn't let go. He just… stared. His hands shook. His breath hitched. He stared at the numbers so long she had to touch his arm to bring him back.

And then, he laughed.

Low. Ragged. Almost hysterical.

"It's real." His voice was barely above a whisper.

She had never seen him look at money like that before. Like it was proof that everything was happening exactly as it should.

The reviews were mixed. Some critics called it derivative but judged it to be "a first effort that requires no apology." Others described it as "an Edgar Allan Poe pastiche."

Still, *The Glass Floor* sold. And with it, something inside him shifted.

Toxicity bled into his daily life, his newfound confidence sharpening into something rigid, something unyielding. He was more assertive, more in control of his thoughts, but at the quiet expense of those around him. The shift was gradual, almost imperceptible at first, but Martha felt it creeping in.

The patience that once softened his edges was wearing thin, the warmth in his presence cooling into something distant, almost mechanical.

The kids noticed first. He still tucked them in at night, still listened when they told him about school, but something was missing. He no longer asked follow-up questions. His goodnight hugs had lost their warmth, more perfunctory than genuine. The smallest shifts. They noticed.

One evening, as Martha was tucking the two of them into bed, their youngest, eyes wide with worry, whispered, "What's wrong with Daddy?"

Martha felt a chill dance along her spine.

"What do you mean, sweetheart?" she asked, brushing hair from their forehead.

"He's… cranky," came the hesitant reply. "Not yelling or anything, but… different."

Their eldest, who had been listening from across the room, chimed in.

"He doesn't play with us like he used to, Mum. He's always busy. And when he talks, it's like… like he's somewhere else."

A small frown settled between their brows.

"Did we do something wrong?"

Martha's stomach twisted.

"No, no," she assured them, her voice softer than she felt inside. "Daddy's just… working hard right now. That's all."

But was it?

Later that night, as she sat at the kitchen table, her tea growing cold, she found herself replaying the past few weeks in her mind. The way he hardly met her gaze anymore unless he had something to say. The way he lingered at the typewriter longer than necessary, even after he had finished his work. How he would stand at the window at odd hours, staring into the dark as if waiting for something.

It wasn't just the kids. She felt it, too. He wasn't cruel. He wasn't angry. But he was different.

She had never known him to be distant, not like this. Not a man physically present but mentally elsewhere, as if some unseen force was pulling his thoughts beyond their home, beyond her, beyond even himself.

She thought of the manuscript. The way it had known things it shouldn't. The way it whispered to her as she read it, as if speaking through him.

And, for the first time since he had started writing, Martha felt afraid.

It was now sometime past midnight when the sound of footsteps padded softly down the hallway.

Martha sat on the couch, curled up with a blanket and a lukewarm cup of tea, the glow of the lamp casting long shadows across the floor. At first, she thought one of the kids was up for water. Then she heard the door creak.

Grace stood in the threshold of the bedroom, her nightgown too thin for the cold, her hair tousled and eyes half-lidded. She didn't look awake, not really.

He stirred in bed, eyes opening slowly, watching as his daughter walked across the room. She stopped beside him, close enough that he could see the pulse in her neck fluttering like a trapped insect. Then she leaned in.

Her voice was a whisper, but it scraped across his spine like broken glass.

"The house is hungry."

His eyes flew open fully. He sat upright, heart thundering.

Martha stepped into the doorway behind Grace, blinking in confusion. "What's going on?" she asked, rubbing sleep from her eyes.

Grace turned toward her mother, still in her trance. She smiled faintly and said, "I'm hungry."

Martha chuckled, bleary. "Then let's get you a snack, sweetheart."

But the struggling writer didn't move. He was staring at his daughter like she'd just spoken in tongues. His notebook was already in his hands, scrawling the words down before they could vanish from his mind.

The house is hungry.

He didn't sleep the rest of the night. Not because he was afraid. But because, for the first time, he wanted to know what it would feed on.

Chapter 4

Feed the Hunger

For the next few months, life settled into a strange illusion of normalcy. Yet, the writer carried himself differently now, no longer struggling, but instead grappling with something new. Imposter syndrome gnawed at him. Am I really a published author? Is that what I can call myself now? He moved through the world with a quiet confidence that almost felt like peace, yet a part of him remained unconvinced. He laughed more, played with the children more, made love to Martha more. At first, she welcomed it. He even spent more time with his mates.

But there was something off about it. Something unsettling, maybe Martha just wasn't used to this side of him. It wasn't all affection, not really. It was almost mechanical, as if something inside him was pulling the strings something that wasn't used to human contact. The passion was there, but so was the detachment. Like he was performing intimacy rather than feeling it. She caught him watching her more than once. Not lovingly. Not lustfully. Just… observing. Studying her closely, as if he were trying to figure something out. Trying to understand. Every time it happened, a little chill ran down her spine. She prayed this version of him would stay. She loved the attention. But deep down, something whispered: He's still changing.

For the new author the words flowed a little more easily this time. There was no hesitation, no frustration, a trust in the process, an unstoppable force driving his fingers over the keys. The clatter of the typewriter filled the house at all hours, each keystroke hammering out something raw, something dark. Something beyond either of them had ever dared think about before, let alone write.

But then, just as quickly, he stopped. Dead in his tracks, crashed and burned like a used puppet that's had a hand stuck up its arse after a long stage performance at the comedy club.

One evening, after hours of writing, out of total frustration that he can't seem to pinpoint why he tore the page from the typewriter, crumpled it into a ball, and threw the whole manuscript straight into the wastepaper basket. A story he's been working on for months.

It was good, but not good enough he thought to himself. The words on the page sat there like a corpse. Flat. Soulless. Wrong.

He leaned back in his chair, staring at the stack of pages as if they might suddenly rewrite themselves. He had pushed and pulled at every sentence, tried to wring something real out of the bones of the story, but it wasn't breathing. It wasn't alive. Frustration coiled inside him, a slow, burning heat creeping up his throat. His fingers twitched. He tried again but in the end he ripped the latest page from the typewriter, crumpled it into a ball, and threw it toward the wastepaper basket. The motion sent a few discarded pages scattering across the floor like fallen leaves.

Martha looked up from the couch, her book half-forgotten in her lap.

"Everything okay?"

No.

The response was on the tip of his tongue, but something held it back.

Instead, he exhaled sharply, rubbing a hand over his face. The trailer suddenly felt too small. The walls felt closer than they should be. "I'm heading to the bar," he muttered, already grabbing his coat. "I'll be back later." Martha barely had time to part her lips before the door slammed shut behind him.

The night air hit him like a slap, cold and sobering.

Good.

Lucky for him the bar was only a few blocks away, his boots struck the pavement in sharp, deliberate steps, each one echoing louder than it should. He shoved his hands into his pockets, gripping the fabric as if to anchor himself, but his thoughts were already unravelling.

It was shit.

No, it wasn't. It just needed time.

Time? You've been at this for years. How much time do you think you have left?

It'll come.

Like it always has? Like it did tonight?

His jaw clenched. He picked up his pace.

The town was empty at this hour, the streetlights buzzing overhead, casting long shadows that flickered when he walked through them. He caught a glimpse of himself in the window of a closed bakery, a reflection that didn't quite match his movements.

He froze mid-step.

Stared.

The face in the glass was his. Of course, it was.

But the eyes.

The light caught them strangely, twisting the colour, warping them just enough to look hollow. Black.

A trick of the glass, the poor lighting.

Still, he looked away.

Kept walking.

You're running out of time.

Shut up.

And yet, you keep throwing it away.

Shut. Up.

The words scratched at the inside of his skull, layered over his own thoughts, but they weren't his.

He wasn't sure when that had started. The second voice. The one that didn't belong.

At first, it was just an echo, a lingering thought that didn't quite feel like his own. Then it was a whisper, curling around the edges of his subconscious like cigarette smoke.

Now?

Now, it was there.

Always.

The neon B in *Bud's Bar & Grill* flickered erratically, half-dead from years of neglect. Inside, the air hung thick with stale beer, old wood, and cigarette smoke that had soaked into the walls for decades.

The author pushed through the door, the sudden warmth washing over him. The usual crowd was scattered across their usual spots, old men hunched over their regrets, younger drunks laughing too loudly at things they wouldn't remember in the morning. Each nodding his general direction as they salute their old friend as he entered the bar.

Behind the bar, polishing a glass with the slow deliberation of a man who'd seen it all, Bud looked up.

The bartender frowned.

"You look like hell. What's wrong?"

The author slid onto the barstool, dropping his coat onto the seat beside him. "Just gimme a drink, Bud." While muttering to himself random thoughts.

Bud didn't move right away. He studied him, like a doctor examining a patient who refused to admit they were sick. Something was different tonight. Bud had never seen him mutter to himself as erratic as this.

Then, without a word, he reached for the whiskey.

A double. Neat.

The glass hit the counter with a soft clink.

"On the house," Bud muttered.

The author didn't argue.

He knocked it back in one go, the burn spreading through his chest, dulling the static in his head. The second drink came without asking. Bud poured slow, watching carefully, the way a man watches a wounded animal to see how he would react.

The alcohol settled in, warm and numbing.

And that's when the voice became clear.

Better, isn't it?

No.

No?

This is just the whiskey talking.

Is it? Or is it me?

The author exhaled sharply, gripping the edge of the bar like it was the only thing keeping him from slipping into the abyss.

But Bud was still watching. Ever closely.

"Listen," the bartender said after a long silence. "You been coming here for years. Never seen you like this. You seem really wound up" Bud notices the writer answering someone who isn't there instead of him.

"I'm fine. He snorted as he looks over his shoulder"

Bud's brow furrowed. He set the glass down, wiping his hands on a rag before reaching for the phone.

"You want me to call Martha?"

The author looked up sharply. "What? No. Jesus, Bud."

"You're talking to yourself," Bud said, his voice quiet so not to tip off any of the other drinkers.

That shut him up. He feels like he's been caught.

A long pause.

Then Bud sighed, rubbing a hand over his bald head. "Look, man. If you need a ride home, I'll order you a cab. But I ain't lettin' you sit here and drown in this. Not like this."

"I'm not drowning."

Bud said nothing.

Because he knew.

The author knew, too.

Something was wrong. And it wasn't the drink.

Despite his protests, Bud walked into the room behind the bar and called Martha. Martha answered on the second ring.

"Hey," Bud said, keeping his voice low. "He's here."

A pause.

"Is he okay?"

Bud glanced at the man slumped over the bar, one hand wrapped around his drink, the other clenching and unclenching like he was trying to hold onto something slipping away.

"He's… not himself," Bud admitted. "But I got him. I'll put him in a cab when he's ready."

Martha exhaled, a mixture of relief and lingering concern. "Thank you."

Bud hung up, pouring himself a drink now. He had a feeling he was going to need one before the night was over.

Martha went over to his writing nook to pick up some of the trash and generally clean up, and was amazed at the amount of beer cans everywhere, taken back she saw packets of white powder hidden under a pile of papers while shuffling papers around. She was furious at first, that arsehole she thought, no wonder his nose bleeds all the time, no wonder he's frantic one minute the nicest guy then the next the worst nightmare. It took Martha everything she had not to go to the bar and string him up for it, flush it down the toilet, for Christ sakes the kids could have found it! but for some reason beyond her, almost like a thought that wasn't her own hinted that she should hold off for now, see how it plays out. She might not be happy but she also recognises that he is his own man and he's pushing himself hard, if this helps then who is she to judge.

Picking up the waste paper basket by the desk she sees that he threw away a half finished manuscript, she hesitated, her hands hovering over the pages most with erratic handwriting across them, but curiosity gnawed at her. She sat down in his chair which smelt like sweat, poor decisions, cigarettes, and alcohol, settling in she started smoothing out the creased paper on the little available desk space, and began to read.

It hooked its claws into her instantly.

The writing was unlike anything he had ever done, more vivid, more violent, more real. She felt herself sink into it, like falling into the mind of something... inhuman. The idea that a young girl's first menstruation could trigger telekinesis, it was unlike anything she had ever read before and Martha was well read, this was new to her.

A sick thrill twisted in her stomach. She knew this was his work… but it felt like something else had written it through him. Is this what he thinks about when he's high on cocaine? She thought to herself.

Martha stayed up most of the night reading the story and woke up to one of the kids looking for her to get some water.

The next day, after the kids had left for school on the bus, Martha was drying the dishes after breakfast watching him recover from the night before with a strong black coffee, she set the manuscript on the counter and slid it toward him.

"I think you should finish this one."

He looked at her, surprised. "Really? I thought it was a loser."

No," she said too quickly. "I read it last night. It's good. Really good.

She saw the flicker of doubt in his eyes. He hadn't planned to finish it. But her insistence seemed to sway him. Even Martha wasn't sure why she had pushed so hard.

In the corner of the room, just beyond the dim light, a pleased Moloch watched on. If you looked a little longer, you might just see his eyes disappear into the smoke from the cigarettes that lingered there a little too long. Moloch was pleased that she found it. He doesn't have his claws in her like he does the author but he can still create events that make her move the way he wants and he's getting stronger the more they interact.

With newfound fervour, he sat at his little desk and reread the manuscript. It took shape faster than anything he had ever written. The words poured out of him, urgent and relentless, as if they had been waiting, clawing at the inside of his skull, desperate to be released. He no longer thought about what he was writing, his fingers moved on their own, hammering at the typewriter keys with a feverish energy that left his knuckles aching and his fingertips raw. Pages piled up beside him, the stack growing taller each night, a monument to something he couldn't quite name.

Martha watched on, silent. He had always worked hard, always pushed himself, but this was different. He no longer muttered frustrations when a sentence didn't land right. He didn't pause to think or rewrite. The usual hesitation, the agonizing self-doubt, gone. It was as if something had taken the wheel of his already over active imagination, driving his hands, guiding his thoughts, and all he could do was keep up. But could he keep up she thought.

He stopped eating at normal hours, skipping meals without noticing. Cigarette smoke curled in thick ribbons around his head, the ashtray overflowing, forgotten. Often he had to stick tissues up his nose as blood constantly poured out from snorting too much cocaine. The trailer reeked of burnt coffee and ink, the scent soaking into everything, even the children's clothes. The kids learned not to disturb him. Martha would find him in the same spot for hours, back hunched, eyes glazed, lips moving silently as he typed.

At night, he didn't so much sleep as collapse. He would wake in strange places, the kitchen table, the couch, once even the floor beside his desk. He couldn't remember getting there. His dreams were filled with distorted faces, whispered voices, shifting landscapes that didn't belong to this world.

And yet, the story was good. really good.

When he read it back, he barely recognized the words. The prose was sharp, alive, humming with something just beneath the surface. It felt like reading a message from something else.

When the final page was typed, he sat back, his body trembling, his breath unsteady. He had finished. He had no memory of writing the last paragraph, but there it was, exactly as it should be.

Martha stepped across the room, arms crossed, eyes scanning the mess of crumpled pages, cigarette butts, and empty beer cans littering the desk. She exhaled, tilting her head. "Well? You gonna sit there staring at it, or are you actually gonna send it off?"

He ran a hand through his hair, still gripping the edge of the desk like it might keep him from floating away. "I don't know," he muttered. "What if it's not as good as I think it is? What if it's just... noise?"

Martha rolled her eyes. "Jesus, you're impossible." She stepped closer, resting a hand on his shoulder. "Look, if you're waiting for some divine sign from the universe that it's perfect, you'll be waiting forever. You finished it. That's the goddamn sign."

He exhaled sharply, tapping his fingers against the desk. "I've sent off a hundred things before, and they always come back with a polite 'thanks but no thanks.' What makes this any different?"

Martha let out a dry chuckle. "Are you serious? Have you actually read what you just wrote?" She picked up the first few pages, flipping through them. "This isn't some throwaway short story. This is it. This is the one. And you know it."

His throat felt tight. He wanted to believe her. Hell, a part of him did believe her. But another part, the part that had lived off rejection letters and self-doubt for years, was screaming at him to hold on a little longer. To tweak a little more. To find an excuse.

Martha saw it in his face. She shook her head, nudging the manuscript toward him. "You always do this. You write something brilliant, and then you convince yourself it's shit. Well, I'm done humouring you." Her voice softened, but there was steel beneath it. "I'll proofread it. I'll retype it. But you are the one who's posting it. No more hiding behind me. No more 'what ifs.' You need to do this for yourself."

He looked at her, the weight of it pressing down on his chest. Then he nodded.

And just like that, he handed the manuscript to her and the hesitation was gone.

A few days after Martha retyped it, she said, "If anything, don't touch it now. Let it dry with the blood still fresh."

He didn't argue. For the first time in a long time, he sent it off without rewriting, without fear. No edits. No doubt.

Just ink, and blood, and whatever else lived between the lines. And she was right.

The response came faster than expected. Major publishers took notice. The rejections that had once piled up, mocking him, never came this time. Tripleday bought the novel, he titled *Caroline*. Unlike his short stories, this was something real. Something big. Not quite a novel, but a fat novella, and that was just fine by him.

For the first time in his life, he felt unstoppable.

The advance check arrived on a beautiful spring afternoon in May 1973.

Martha found him in the kitchen, the letter in one hand, the cheque in the other, his fingers trembling. This was big, bigger than the first check he got for *The Glass Floor*, this was real money. Life changing money. This one check was nearly six month's salary, and that's not counting the royalties he'll soon get.

For the first time in his life, his dream, their dream was real.

Outside, in the shadowed corners of their quiet neighbourhood, something waited. Moloch. Just beyond the light. Just beyond reality was taking hold in the dark places of his reality not just his mind, but his neighbourhood too.

And it was pleased. Very pleased.

With the success of *Caroline*, things changed overnight.

The new to them house on Maple Street stood tall and proud beneath the afternoon sun, its white paint gleaming, its small front porch stretching out like a welcoming embrace. The For Sale sign was gone now, replaced by the weight of ownership, of permanence.

The kids tumbled out of the car before the engine had even fully stopped.

"I get the biggest room!" their eldest shouted, racing toward the front door.

"No fair!" the youngest protested, scrambling after his sister, their voices echoing across the quiet street.

Martha laughed, shaking her head as she stepped out of the passenger seat. She turned to him, her eyes shining in the golden light.

"Well," she said, a smile teasing at her lips. "We did it."

He exhaled, looking up at the house, their house, taking it all in. The sheer size of it compared to the trailer they had lived in for the past year. The way the windows caught the light. The two-car garage at the back. The yard that stretched out into actual space, not just a postage stamp of land with a rusted lawn chair and broken toys scattered about.

It felt surreal. They had lived in tiny apartments, rented spaces with thin walls and ceilings that leaked when it rained. They had scraped by, pay check to pay check, hoping, praying, that something would change.

And now, here they were.

The sound of the historical front door creaking open yanked him from his thoughts.

"Whoa!" their eldest gasped from inside. "This place is huge!"

Boots scuffed against hardwood floors as the kids darted through the hallway, their laughter filling the space, bouncing off the walls. The echoes made it feel more empty than full, but that would change. Soon, it would be their home, lived in, broken in, cluttered with everyday mess.

Martha turned to him, still standing beside the car, a quiet kind of awe settling over her face.

"Are you gonna just stand there, or are you gonna help me unload?" she teased.

He let out a breathy chuckle, running a hand through his hair. "I don't know. I kinda just want to look at it for a minute."

Martha followed his gaze. The house was fancy, and it was theirs. A four-bedroom home in a quiet neighbourhood where the kids could ride their bikes, where she could finally have her own little reading nook, where he could shut himself away in an office that wasn't just a cluttered corner of a trailer.

He turned to her, then, really looked at her. The exhaustion, the years of sacrifice, the quiet hope in her expression. He walked over to her, still leaning against the old Buick he reached out, pulling her in, wrapping his arms around her in a rare, full-bodied embrace.

She melted into him, sighing against his shoulder.

"I'm proud of you," she murmured.

His grip tightened slightly. "I wouldn't have done it without you."

She pulled back just enough to meet his eyes. "You're damn right you wouldn't have."

He smirked, shaking his head, before pressing a kiss to her temple.

From inside, a crash sounded, probably a suitcase knocked over in the race for bedroom claims, followed by the shriek of their youngest.

"That's my room!"

"Too late! I licked the door!"

"Oh, gross!"

Martha groaned, pulling away. "Well. The peace and quiet was nice while it lasted."

He chuckled, picking up the nearest box from the trunk. "Welcome home, then."

She grinned, grabbing one of her own. "Yeah. Welcome home."

And together, they stepped through the front door.

But with the bigger house came more space for the shadows to hide.

His fame grew. Newspapers called him "a fresh new voice in horror." Reviews raved about his prose. Critics likened him to Bram Stoker, Poe, Lovecraft. But he found no real joy in it. He wanted more.

Instead, something else grew inside him, a hunger, a compulsion. He wrote more than ever, barely sleeping, his new big desk still covered in ashtrays overflowing with cigarette butts and more beer cans than you can buy in a case. Scraps of paper littered the floor, filled with disjointed sentences and cryptic messages in frantic handwriting.

The bookshop was small, tucked between a closed-down cinema and a pawn shop that hadn't changed its window display in a decade. Inside, the air smelled like yellowed paper and old wood polish. The signing table sat beneath a handmade banner that read: ***Welcome Local Author of "Caroline"!***

He sat with a pen in hand, trying to force a smile each time someone approached. Most of them were polite, thrilled even. Locals. Teachers. Retirees. A woman in a heavy knit scarf asked if he taught at the high school. A young man with acne nervously told him he wanted to write one day too.

Then came the final figure. A man in a grey coat, wiry and pale, eyes too wide and unblinking. He didn't say anything at first. Just placed a well-worn copy of *The Glass Floor* on the table.

The author looked down. Every single page had been annotated in tiny, cramped handwriting. Symbols had been drawn in the margins, circles and arrows, obscure runes, lines connecting passages across chapters.

"This is… thorough," he said, forcing a laugh.

The man finally spoke, voice raspy and low. "It's not fiction. It's a map."

A silence fell between them. One of the bookshop staff called out that it was time to wrap up, but the author didn't look away from the man.

"You drew these?" he asked, tapping the symbols.

"No. I just found them," the man replied. "But you wrote them."

Something in the air shifted. It was cold, just for a second. The author's fingertips tingled where they touched the page.

"Keep it," the man said. "You'll need it for the next one."

Then he turned and walked out, disappearing into the street like he'd never been there at all.

Martha kept editing his work, careful not to change too much, that was for the publisher. But her fears grew. She had watched him struggle for years, desperate for success. Now he had it… yet he was drinking himself into oblivion. And it wasn't the alcohol consuming him, it was the hunger.

His next novel came faster than the first. Start to finish within a year.

He barely remembered writing it. The words spilled out in an unstoppable flood, the typewriter keys hammering out something he couldn't take back.

But this time, something changed.

The nightmares came back. Fear of being violent to those he loved was driving his thoughts and actions.

Shadowy figures lurked at the edges of his vision. He dreamed of places that should not exist. Buildings that breathed, roads that bled, faces without eyes. Martha doesn't like the corner in the laundry room. She says it stares at her.

He woke up gasping, drenched in sweat, the taste of blood in his mouth from his nose bleeds.

He started drinking more heavily, trying to quiet the whispers that echoed through the house at night.

"Why is Daddy acting weird again?" their youngest asked one evening.

Martha tried to brush it off. "He's just working really hard."

But even she didn't believe it.

One night, she woke up alone. The bed was empty.

She found him sitting at his typewriter, staring at a blank page.

His fingers hovered over the keys, but he wasn't typing.

His lips were moving. Whispering.

A low, rhythmic chant. Words she didn't recognize. Words she didn't want to understand.

Despite genuine fear enveloping her thoughts She stepped closer. "Honey?"

His hands snapped into fists. He blinked hard, like shaking off a trance, then looked at her as he reached out and gripped her wrist a little too hard.

His face was different.

For a split second, it was like she didn't recognize him at all.

Then as he released his grip he smiled, the same warm smile she had always known.

"Couldn't sleep," he murmured. "Had a scene stuck in my head."

Martha forced a laugh. "Well, don't let it drive you crazy."

He chuckled, but as she walked back toward the bedroom, she heard the clatter of the typewriter start again.

Click-clack. Click-clack. Click-clack.

Faster. Urgent. Desperate.

And then, a whisper.

Not his.

From the corner of the room.

From the dark.

Martha turned back, but he was alone.

The next morning, the outline for *Bethlehem's Lot* was finished. The fastest he's ever done.

It would be published later that year.

His second book. His second success.

But as he sat at the kitchen table, staring down at the contract, his hands shook.

He knew it now. Knew it completely.

The words were no longer his own.

And Moloch was just getting started. The air in the kitchen thickened, the fluorescent light overhead flickering once, twice, before cutting out entirely. He felt it first, the sensation of being watched, something just outside his field of vision. Then he looked up and Moloch was there. Sitting across from him in his fucking kitchen, hands folded, as if they had been having a polite conversation all along.

Chapter 5

On the Road

The book deal for "*Caroline*" should have felt like salvation for him. It should have lifted the weight that had been pressing down on him for years. And for a while, it did. The money certainly helped. The recognition helped. People wanted to hear what he had to say. And the papers want to know whose shirts he wears. They wanted to shake his hand, hear his thoughts, call him brilliant. But even as the world opened up to him, something inside him closed tighter. The more they celebrated him, the less real he felt.

And the dreams kept coming. Not fleeting nightmares...no, these were visions. Persistent. Familiar. Places that should not exist yet felt more real than the ground beneath his feet. A library of human-skin-bound books with eyes blinking on the spines, wondering if he'll save them from their prison, their pages shifting and writhing as he reads them. A hallway of endless doors, some cracked open, revealing glimpses of grotesque landscapes...a sky made of teeth, a city pulsing like a beating heart. A faceless man, standing just behind him, whispering in words he could never remember when he woke.

Moloch was always there now. Watching. Waiting. He never acknowledged Moloch when Martha or the kids were around but he started to talk more openly to him, asking questions, getting ideas. The whispers in his head weren't his own anymore. He knows that now. They had started like echoes, barely distinguishable from his own thoughts. Then they became clearer. More confident. They weren't suggestions anymore. They were becoming commands.

Along with this he started losing time. At first, it was only a few minutes. He'd be writing, blink, and suddenly, the clock had jumped forward. Then the gaps stretched...an hour gone, a whole afternoon vanished. He'd wake up to pages stacked neatly beside him, written in his own hand, but the words were not his. The stories disturbed even him. The prose was alive, sentences twisting with feverish energy. Characters on the page moved without him telling them to. Themes bled through the pages that he hadn't intended. Ideas he had never thought of emerged, fully formed, crawling out of his typewriter like things trying to escape.

Martha found the discarded scraps of notes written in frantic handwriting, his, to be sure, but clearly rushed and almost incompressible. She tried to piece them together, but the words didn't make sense. Some weren't even in English. Some were nothing but symbols, spirals that made her dizzy when she stared at them too long like they're trying to hypnotise her, suggest things to her. Possess her. When she confronted him, he just smiled, that perfect smile she was beginning to resent. "They're just ideas, babe. Just scraps of ideas." But he wasn't sleeping. He wasn't eating. He wasn't himself. She's starting to miss his old self.

His debut book tour was meant to have been exhilarating. His name was everywhere. People lined up at signings, clutching copies of *Caroline* with reverence. Critics hailed him as a new voice in horror, the next Poe, the next Lovecraft, the next King of Horror. He felt nothing though, numb. Not what he expected. A hollow feeling that keeps growing with every interaction, with every book he signed. On some level loved it all, relished it even, but his hunger to write more and more was overwhelming.

He started to even write lines in books instead of dedicating them "To Sarah, hope you enjoy this..." instead he wrote "The town cares for devil's work no more than it cares for God's or man's. It knew darkness. And darkness was enough". The attention started to suffocated him, started to tempt him. Young women would ask him to sign their breasts while flashing him in the bookstore, others would leave a room key for him with explicit instructions. And on top of all that the pressure to produce the next book clawed at his chest. He wasn't just writing anymore...he was compelled to. He could feel it inside him, a gnawing hunger that wasn't his own.

The drinking and cocaine was a way to calm his nerves. Then, it was a way to numb the voices so he could have a normal dialogue with Moloch, hear him properly. The pills came next... He convinced himself they were just something to help him sleep. Then something to keep him awake. He stopped keeping track. He stopped caring.

Things started to fray in little ways, to an outsider they may not have even noticed anything wrong, to those that knew him personally, it was obvious something was taking hold. During a reading in Chicago, he zoned out mid-sentence. He had been halfway through a particularly gruesome passage, the audience hanging on his every word, and then…

He blinked. Silence. He was staring at the last page of the chapter. The audience started clapping. He must have finished the reading, but he had no memory of doing so. Someone in the front row caught his eye, their brows furrowed. Had they noticed? Had he just been reading mechanically, eyes unfocused, mouth moving on its own? The applause sounded wrong... distant, warped, like it was coming from the bottom of a well. Then, just beneath the noise, he heard his name. Whispered. But no one had spoken. His fingers clenched the edges of the podium. His head turned slightly, scanning the crowd. He could feel it...someone watching him. His vision blurred, and for just a second, the audience shifted. The rows of people twisted like an old film reel burning up in the projector.

And there, standing in the back of the room, was a sexy vintage lady leaning on Moloch's shoulder. Standing tall and proud of the work he's doing. His silhouette was unmistakable. Dressed in a simple dark three piece suit, head slightly tilted, his black, bottomless eyes locked onto him. The author blinked. Gone. The applause returned to normal. The audience was still there, still staring, still waiting. He forced a smile. Laughed it off. Turned the page. But his hands were shaking. His publicists leaned into his ear saying "ground control to Major Tom" you drifted off for a second there, you ok? Yeah, yeah I'm ok, I just thought I saw someone I knew. I think I need a drink.

As with all these affairs reporters follow the circus that is a whirlwind book tour. The headline read "Is the King of Horror Losing His Grip on Reality?" (An article by Daniel Kessler, Daily Defender, January 1975.)

Is the King of Horror Losing His Grip on Reality?

By Daniel Kessler

There was a time when novelists were simply writers. Now, they are rock stars. Take the case of our newest literary sensation, a man whose debut horror novel, *Caroline*, has taken the world by storm. His name is on every horror reader's lips, and his book is flying off shelves faster than bookstores can stock them. But behind the hype, the signings, and the late-night talk show appearances, something is... wrong.

For the past four weeks, I have been on the road with him, trailing the growing media circus that surrounds his every move. I expected to find a man enjoying his success...an overwhelmed but thriving talent, adjusting to newfound fame. What I found was something else entirely. He doesn't sleep. Not really. He collapses. I have watched him drift off in the back of limousines, his head lolling to the side as if someone had flipped a switch...only to jolt awake minutes later, drenched in sweat, his eyes darting as if he had seen something the rest of us could not.

At signings, he smiles, shakes hands, and poses for photos. But something is off. His eyes flicker from face to face too quickly, as if searching for someone...or avoiding someone. And then there are the things he writes in his adoring fan's books. Passages from stories he hasn't published. Sentences that seem wrong...not just eerie, but foreign. One young woman opened her signed copy to find the words: "The ones who walk behind the paper will not let you leave." She laughed nervously, but I saw the way he stared at the page afterward, as if he hadn't realized he had written it.

Then there are the disappearances. Three cities so far. A girl went missing after a signing in Chicago. A bartender in Albuquerque. A bellboy at the hotel in Dallas. They were there. And then they weren't. I asked him about it once, casually, over drinks. He blinked, confused, as if hearing about it for the first time. Then, very softly, he said: "People disappear all the time." And he smiled. Now, I sit in his hotel lobby, waiting for another signing to begin, wondering if I should even be writing this article. Fame changes people. But this isn't just fame. This is something else. Something is very wrong with him. And if I'm being honest? I'm afraid to ask what.

One night, after a reading in New Mexico, the author woke up in a hotel bathtub. Fully clothed. Drenched in cold sweat. He had no idea how he got there. In the mirror above the sink, a message was scrawled in red lipstick:

MORE. WRITE MORE.

He climbed out of the tub and leaned against the sink, hands trembling as he fumbled with the tap, watching the water run. Clear, clean, pointless. The light above buzzed like a dying insect. He splashed his face, hoping it would snap him back to something solid. It didn't.

Then, without asking permission, a memory surfaced.

The dinner table. The kids still young. Grace poking at her peas with a fork oversized for her hand. Martha laughing... God, that laugh... full-throated, careless. Not the brittle sound it would later become. The trailer warm with baked pasta and cheap red wine. A storm chewing at the windows outside. He was talking about deadlines. About editors. About how no one gave a shit about short stories anymore unless they had sex or murder by page three.

'You need a break,' Martha had said, pouring him another glass. Her hand brushed his arm, a small gesture, but real. Solid. 'Go with your friends this weekend. You haven't seen them in months. We'll be fine here. The kids are dying to try that new board game anyway.'

He'd smiled then. A real one. Or what passed for it. Told her he'd think about it.

But he didn't go for the break. Not really. He went because the silence in the house had taken on an edge. Because their daughter had asked, 'Why does Daddy look tired all the time?' and Martha had flinched like she'd been struck.

And now?

Now the memory was back, curling around the rot that festered behind his eyes. But it wasn't warm anymore. It twisted. His mind pulled the threads loose... Martha's laugh echoed with a false brightness; Grace's voice grated; the storm outside no longer comforting, but hungry.

He braced himself on the counter, the mirror a fractured version of his own face. He remembered the pasta. Remembered thinking it needed salt. How smug they all looked, trying so hard to be happy.

He should've stayed home. Should've played that board game. Shouldn't have taken that goddamn break at the lake.

Instead, he let something in.

And now he couldn't get it out.

He was alone in the room. Or so he told himself. He had vague memories of a peculiar young woman who seemed to be infatuated with his every move. He saw her at every event, every party, every book signing. Was this lipstick note on the mirror a message from her? He couldn't think of anything more miserable than an infatuated stalker. So much so it planted the seed for a new story in his mind. As he undressed to get into the shower, to his surprise, he found the lipstick in his own pocket.

He was still rattled when he got to the next event. A co-signing with some midlist horror guy named James Vale. Small venue, indie vibe. Folding tables and paperbacks stacked in crooked towers. The kind of place that smelled like mildew and ambition.

They sat side by side behind a makeshift table, a poster hanging above them that made both their names look far more important than either of them felt. Between signings, Vale kept glancing over at him. Not in awe. More like… recognition. Like a man watching someone step into a role he'd once auditioned for and barely survived.

They'd only just started the signing, but already Vale was talking too much, in that way people do when the silence between them starts to stretch long enough to feel dangerous.

'You ever get hand cramps from signing your own name so many times?' Vale muttered, scrawling his signature across a glossy cover without looking. 'Feels like I'm forging myself into oblivion.'

He chuckled but didn't wait for a response.

'I miss when this was a dream. Before it became a fuckin' admin job.'

Our author gave a polite nod, eyes drifting to the queue, avoiding the stack of books bearing his name in embossed letters.

'You've got that look, y'know,' Vale went on. 'Like it's still new to you. But not in a good way.'

He glanced sideways again. 'Wide-eyed. Like you've seen behind the curtain and it didn't make you wise… just dependent.'

That earned a sideways glance. 'Thanks.'

Vale smirked. 'Don't worry. We all start that way. First taste of fame and you think you've won the lotto. But really, you've just been seen… and now they're watching.'

Another book slid across the table. Another fake smile.

'You seen her yet?' Vale finally asked, flipping the cap off a pen with his thumbnail.

'Who?'

'Tall. Pale. Red lipstick. Looks like she stepped out of an old photo and didn't quite dry off.'

He raised an eyebrow. 'You talking about a fan?'

Vale chuckled. 'I don't think she reads.' He paused, his tone flattening. 'But she shows up. Always shows up. Different cities. Same woman. Doesn't need a pass. Doesn't queue. Just… appears. Close enough to smell. You'll know when it's her.'

Now it was his turn to smirk. 'And what, she asks for a signature?'

Vale's eyes darkened.

'No. She the type that just gets in the car. Fucks you like she's trying to rip something out of you. Then vanishes.'

He gave a dry laugh, but his hand trembled slightly as he reached into his pocket. He pulled out a napkin... old, soft, almost translucent from the oils of time. A single lipstick print bloomed in the centre. Beneath it, scrawled in faint red ink: *You'll write better now.*

He slid it over without looking. 'She only comes to the ones dared look into the abyss and somehow they've let something in.'

The line of fans moved, books shuffled forward, and neither of them said anything for a beat.

Then Vale's head tilted.

'Don't look now,' he muttered, 'but…'

He nodded towards the back of the queue.

There she was.

Tall. Pale. Hair like black thread caught in the rain. Blood-red lips. No badge. No book. Just standing there, calm, as if the queue had formed around her.

And suddenly, there it was... that scent. A faint trace on the air. Unplaceable. Not perfume. Not sweat. Something sweet and burnt and rotten all at once, like singed flowers wilted in a vase over a humid spell.

He followed Vale's gaze. Their eyes met... uncertain. Recognition. Disbelief.

They looked back.

Gone.

Nothing but a gap in the line, a yawning absence.

And just behind it, a man halfway down the queue lit another cigarette. The smoke curled upward in lazy swirls, the shape of something exhaled, or maybe leaving.

He looked back at them... confused. Like he wasn't sure why they were staring at him. Like they'd seen something he hadn't.

Vale swallowed.

'You saw her, right?'

He didn't answer.

Didn't need to.

Martha tried calling again while he was on the road. He didn't often answer the phone. When he did pick up, he was slurring, incoherent. Sometimes, she could hear people in the background, music playing, strangers laughing, voices deep and distorted.

For Martha, the first real sign that he was in trouble came when his agent called her directly. 'We found him passed out at the table,' they said. 'He wouldn't wake up at first.' Martha swallowed hard, gripping the phone. 'Did he... did he say anything when he woke up?' A pause. A hesitation. Then, in a quiet voice: 'He kept saying someone was in the room with him.' Martha didn't ask who. She already knew. This thing is taking hold.

Martha sat on the edge of the bed, legs tucked under her dressing gown, the phone with its 20ft cord idle in her lap. She stared at the muted television across the room, some rerun flickering in the dark, the sound turned down low enough it barely existed.

The kids were asleep. The house, hollow.

He hadn't picked up. Again.

She reached for the wine glass on the nightstand, its rim stained with lipstick, and took a sip that had lost whatever warmth it once had. It tasted like something that used to be fruit with ambition.

He was in another city. Signing books. Shaking hands. Getting photographed next to women pretending to read horror for the thrill of proximity. And she, she was here. Toothbrush in hand, scrubbing glitter glue off the tiles. School lunches. Permission slips. Homework. Routines.

But if it hadn't been for her...

She'd sent the manuscript. *Caroline.* The battered folder he'd abandoned. Left buried in a drawer beneath tax returns and forgotten bills. She'd opened it. Sorted the pages. Retyped the salvageable bits. Even rewrote a few sections where the words had collapsed in on themselves, half-baked thoughts scrawled at three in the morning, stinking of desperation and cheap bourbon. Just suggestions, at first. Then whole paragraphs. Polishing. Sharpening. Saving it from itself.

And now?

He was the King of Horror.

A bitter laugh escaped, dry as dust, and she drained the glass.

She hadn't told him. Of course not. What could she say? That the line everyone quoted, *'I was never your daughter, only your reflection'*, had come to her while folding washing? That the second act twist had bloomed in her mind in the supermarket queue, somewhere between tinned tomatoes and tampons?

No. He wouldn't hear it. Not now. Not with everything in his life suddenly gilded and screaming with significance. No room for other voices. Only his. And Moloch's.

She crossed the room, switched off the television with the back of her hand. The screen went black, and for a moment her reflection stared back, flat, drawn, eyes that didn't blink.

Jealousy curled in her stomach like something old and hungry. Not about the money, or the tours, or the fanfare. It was the myth of it. The way the world had decided he was born brilliant. As if talent had fallen into his lap like a gift from the void. No one saw the patchwork. No one saw what was stitched together in the quiet hours, while he slept, or raged, or vanished into another spiral.

She pulled the curtains and killed the light.

Let him have it. Let him bathe in applause and praise. One day, he'd remember what he forgot. What wasn't his. What came from her.

And when that day arrived, she wasn't sure if she wanted gratitude... or his bones.

The room fell dark, the only glow now from the television's afterburn across the glass screen, slow to fade. Martha turned away from it, exhaled, and slipped beneath the covers, the phone still cradled in her hand like a relic from a better time.

She didn't see the shape in the corner.

But we did.

A tall figure, stitched from absence, nested in the shadows near the dresser. Head tilted. Watching.

Moloch.

He stood utterly still, hands clasped behind his back, the way men do at funerals when they've run out of lies. His black eyes shimmered like oil beneath a dying star. He didn't move, didn't speak.

But he smiled.

Not at her.

At us.

As if he knew what she'd done. What she hadn't said. As if her silence was just another verse in the story he'd already written.

The screen finally blinked to black.

And so did he.

He got drunk again after a reading one night. Stumbling back into his hotel room, he caught his reflection in the window. At first, he thought it was just him... just his own shadow. But the longer he stared, the more he realised it wasn't moving when he did. Moloch stood behind him, just outside the edges of the light. Smiling. He didn't turn around. He just whispered, 'What do you want from me?' The shadow's head tilted, black pits where eyes should have been. You already know. We have a pact, you and I. Don't you remember?

Martha sat on the edge of their bed back home, the phone gripped tight in her hands. She had just finished another call... another hotel, another night of bad news. She stared at the floor, her heart heavy, knowing that whatever had taken hold of her husband was only getting stronger. He was losing himself. And she didn't know how to bring him back. But she had to try. She had to. Before there was nothing left of him at all.

About two weeks after he returns home, his constant pacing, restless, searching for anything to fill the void, is wearing everyone thin. The house feels smaller with him inside it, his presence heavy and unsettled. Martha watches him drift from room to room like a ghost and knows something has to change.

"We need to get away," she tells him one evening, her voice measured, careful. "Just us. No distractions. Just… breathe for a while."

They settle on Colorado, a random place with no history for either of them, no significance, no ghosts of the past clinging to it. The kids are sent off to friends' houses, and with nothing but a hastily packed suitcase and the thin hope that distance might be enough, they head for the Rocky Mountains.

They found the Berkley Hotel just as it was closing for the season but they let them stay for three nights before they might get snowed in. It felt creepy even for them, the only two breathing souls in the dining hall.

While sitting there eating dinner in the grand hall all on their own, Martha makes him promise to remain clean but like all junkies he agrees to pacify, not to comply. One thing Martha has been struggling with is a line that one of the rehab nurses told her in private when he was in rehab last time. "Once a junkie, always a junkie" and to "come to terms that all junkies are good liars, take everything as a lie unless you can prove it to be true". This reality hit Martha hard. At first she refused to believe that he would so brazenly lie to her but time and time again he has. She's starting to read him better, see what his "tells" are, she is bracing herself that one day she'll find him and he won't come back.

While out at the Berkley Hotel he had an idea for a story, one that was going to help him work through some of his darkest secrets. After writing *"The Boy"* he realised that he could use his writing as a method of dealing with fears, phobias, and childhood trauma, a way he hoped that would replace his cocaine habit.

On Saturday night, sleep eluded him. The silence of the empty 140-room hotel pressed in, thick and suffocating. Restless, he wandered the halls, following the dim glow of exit signs until he found himself at the bar. A lone bartender, Brady, poured him a drink, his voice low and measured as he spun tales of the hotel's past.

The stories slithered into his mind, curling around his thoughts like smoke. By the time he stumbled back to his room, an idea had taken root, dark and inescapable.

Back home, the hotel lingered in his mind. It became the stage for something much larger, something monstrous. He sat down to write, and the words poured out, cosmic horror, paranoia, the slow unravelling of sanity. But beneath the fiction, beneath the ghosts and shadows, he knew what it really was. A confession. Finishing the rough draft left him hollow. He stared at the pages, knowing he had put something real onto paper, something that perhaps should have stayed buried. But when his friends invited him to the lake, the manuscript came with him. And after a few drinks, when they begged for a story, he didn't hesitate. He decides to read to them the draft of his latest novel "The Shimmering". Even Martha hasn't seen this one. This one is personal, deliberate, and raw. After finishing the first chapter there is just silence. No chuckle. No response. Just a gap in time until finally, Mike exclaims, WHAT THE FUCK?

Chapter 6

Intermission

He woke on the cold floor of his office again, his cheek pressed against a sheet of paper, ink smudged against his skin like a brand. His fingers were stiff, curled into claws, dried blood crusted beneath his nose. The air was thick with the scent of cigarettes, sweat, and something else, something wet and decomposing. Something's wrong. Oh fuck, I shit my pants," he murmured to himself. The dim light from the desk lamp flickered, casting warped shadows against the walls. Crumpled pages surrounded him, a graveyard of discarded thoughts, rejected ideas. The typewriter sat in front of him, its last word frozen on the page, an unfinished sentence, a thought severed in motion.

He didn't remember writing it. Didn't remember last night. Or the one before, hell it's been a while since he's remembered much of anything. The gaps in his memory were widening, stretching into black holes. The words on the page were not his, yet they came from his fingers. His body ached as he pushed himself upright, his head swimming. He sat up slow. Every joint ached. The room spun sideways. The window was open, though he had no memory of opening it. The curtains billowed, the cool night air slithering in, bringing with it the whispering wind. But beneath it, beneath the rustling leaves and creaking branches, there was something else. A voice. No, not a whisper anymore. A harmonious chorus of screams.

"More."

His vision swam as he stumbled toward the door, nearly tripping over the empty whiskey bottles and pill containers littering the floor. The whispers followed him, creeping under his skin. They slithered into his ears, coiling around his brain, sinking their claws deeper into his subconscious. He had ignored them before, dismissed them as exhaustion, stress, or the side effects of too much cocaine. But now, they had become a constant.

The first time he saw the writing on the walls, he thought it was a joke. Red lipstick. Scrawled across the peeling wallpaper in frantic, jagged strokes. At first, they were just short phrases, fragments of his own work, lines from stories he hadn't yet written. Then came the symbols. The spirals. The twisting, shifting patterns that made his stomach churn when he stared at them too long. A language he did not understand. A language that had no business existing in this world.

Then, one morning, he woke up in his car.

He was in the middle of an empty field, miles from home. The sunrise bled across the horizon in hues of crimson and gold, the morning mist curling low over the earth. A notepad sat in the passenger seat, pages stacked neatly beside it. His hands shook as he picked it up, flipping through the pages. The letters shifted, twisted, reformed into something unreadable the longer he focused. The harder he tried to make sense of them, the louder the whispers became. A sharp pain lanced through his skull, and then his nose was bleeding again, the warm trickle slipping over his lips.

He shoved the pages into the glovebox and drove home in silence.

Martha was waiting for him at the door, arms crossed, her face tight with worry and exhaustion. "Where the hell have you been?" Her voice trembled between anger and fear. "I don't know," he admitted, rubbing his face, smearing blood across his chin. The nightmares had broken into waking life now. He confessed to Martha that he had been hearing things, seeing things he could not explain. At first, the voices had been nothing more than echoes in the back of his mind, faint whispers nudging him forward as he wrote. Encouraging. Coaxing. But then they had changed. They had grown insistent. Demanding.

"Not enough. MORE."

They followed him everywhere now. At the dinner table. In the shower. In bed. He stopped using mirrors.

Moloch was there now. In the reflections. Not just glimpses, not tricks of the light. He lingered. Watching. Waiting. His reflection was wrong, delayed by a second, a blink behind, a grin that stretched wider than it should have. One night, he woke with his own fingernails dug deep into his forearms, crescent moons carved into his skin, raw and red. He had been gripping himself in his sleep. Holding himself down. Something had been inside him. Something had been trying to get out.

Martha often found him hunched over his desk, unshaven, his shirt stained with sweat and ink, his fingers hovering over the typewriter keys, unmoving. He wasn't writing. He was just... sitting there, staring at the blank page, waiting.

Martha had seen the changes. Felt them. In the way he walked, in the way he spoke, when he even spoke at all. But most of all, she saw it in the way he was with the kids.

It started small, subtle enough that she convinced herself it was nothing. A hand that lingered too long on their shoulders, not in affection, but in restraint. A tight grip on an arm when they were playing rough. A snap in his voice that carried more venom than the situation called for.

Then, one night, it was more than that.

She had been folding laundry in the bedroom when she heard the sharp, startled cry from the living room. Not the playful whine of a child losing a game, but something else. Something wrong. She dropped the clothes and rushed out.

Alex stood frozen, his little hands clutching his wrist, his face scrunched up in confusion and pain. Grace was wide-eyed, standing behind the couch like a witness too scared to speak.

He stood over them, his chest rising and falling in sharp bursts, his fingers curled into fists. The static hum of the television filled the silence.

Martha took a step forward before she even knew what she was doing. "What happened?"

The author's head jerked up like he hadn't realised she was there. His pupils were engulfing their sockets, swallowing the colour in his eyes. He looked at Alex, at his own hands , staring like they didn't belong to him. Then back at her, blinking rapidly, like he was waking up mid-nightmare.

"He wouldn't sit still," he muttered. His voice was distant, disconnected. Like he wasn't really there. Instead, something in his place.

Martha rushed to Alex's side, gently pulling his wrist toward her. There, on the soft skin, a bruise was already forming, her husband's fingerprints etched into their son's flesh.

For a moment, all she could do was stare at the mark, her mind blank with the weight of it. The undeniable proof.

Grace spoke then, her voice barely above a whisper.

"Daddy scared us."

The room went deathly quiet.

Her husband exhaled sharply, dragging a hand down his face. "I didn't mean to, " He stopped himself, squeezing his temples as if he could pinch the memory out of his skull.

Martha slowly looked up at him. Not the man she married. Not anymore. She saw the weight in his shoulders, the darkness in his eyes that had nothing to do with exhaustion. There was something else living inside him, something wearing his skin like an ill-fitting suit. And for the first time, she realised she wasn't just worried.

She was afraid.

She turned to the kids, her voice as steady as she could make it. "Go to your rooms."

Grace grabbed Alex's hand, pulling him away quickly. Neither of them protested.

The author opened his mouth like he wanted to say something, to explain, to excuse, but Martha was already stepping past him.

She walked into the kitchen, turned off the stove where dinner had been simmering, wiped her hands on a dish towel. She needed to breathe, to collect herself before she,

No.

There was no collecting herself. Not anymore.

She turned back, walking slowly toward the office, her feet moving before her mind caught up.

He was sitting at his desk, hunched over, staring at the blank page before him. Fingers twitching, as if even now, even after what he had just done, he wanted to write instead of face what had happened.

Martha didn't hesitate.

She placed a gentle hand on his shoulder, her touch hesitant, like she was afraid he might shatter beneath it.

"I can't do this anymore."

He flinched. The words hit him harder than a slap. His eyes darted to her, desperate, pleading.

"No. No, Martha, please." His voice cracked. "I'll get better. I swear to God, I'll get better."

His words were empty, and Martha knew it.

She had heard every version of this lie before, each one worn thinner than the last. And just like always, there was no conviction behind them. Just panic. Just the instinct of a man who couldn't bear to be alone, but had already let himself become a stranger.

She grabbed his face, forcing him to look at her.

"I don't know what's worse, the way you look at me like I'm a stranger, or the way you don't look at me at all."

His eyes were hollow, the irises swallowed by darkness, his pupils wide and devouring. His skin had taken on a strange pallor, his cheekbones sharper, his body thinner, his beard thicker like a werewolf was forcing its way out of him. Something in him had decayed, something vital had rotted away.

Martha's breath hitched, her hands shaking. "You're not even here, are you?"

The lights flickered. The room grew smaller. She wiped her tears and stepped back. Then, without another word, she grabbed the kids and walked out the front door. Carrying nothing but her dignity.

He didn't follow.

For a long time, he just sat there, staring at the door. The silence in the house was different now, no longer just the absence of sound but the presence of something vast, something empty. A black hole had formed. It settled into his bones, pressed against his chest, made it hard to breathe. They were gone. Really gone. A sharp, stinging pain crept into his throat, an ache he hadn't felt in years. He clutched the arms of his chair, his nails digging into the worn wood. He should chase after them. He should fix this. He should, A slow scraping sound. From across the desk, something slid into view. A small, familiar packet, the fine white powder shifting inside like restless ghosts. "You can let it all out now," Moloch murmured from the shadows. His breath came in short, ragged bursts. His fingers twitched, reaching out instinctively before curling into a fist.

No.

But the pain inside him clawed at his ribs, ripped through his veins, turned every inch of him inside out. His head pounded, his hands shook, and the weight of the emptiness threatened to break him apart.

He loosened his fist. With trembling fingers, he picked up the packet, tore it open, and dipped a fingernail inside. The powder clung to it, waiting. A second of hesitation, of clarity, of knowing this would only drag him deeper. But what was the alternative? Feeling it?

No. In one quick inhale, it was gone. The burn seared through his sinuses, a sharp sting that dissolved into something warm, something light. His body sagged, his head lolling back against the chair as the rush swept through him like a tide, pulling him under. His lips parted, and he let go. Just as Moloch asked.

The drugs took over. A binge like no other. Cocaine, whiskey, pills, mouthwash to rinse and repeat. It didn't matter. It was all the same. He wrote for three days straight. No food. No water. His fingers bled onto the typewriter keys, smudging the paper with red. The words poured out of him, as if they had been waiting. But they weren't his. They were Moloch's.

The story unfolded on its own, a thing that had been buried inside him, clawing its way free. He was just the vessel. His body was weakening. His mind was fraying. He could feel it. He was dying. Something else was being born.

Ripping the last page he wrote out of the typewriter he reads over the page not convinced it was good enough…

Darren Grick lay in bed, the blankets tangled around his legs, his breath shallow in the silence of the room. The night pressed in, thick and oppressive, the air heavy with something unseen. Moonlight slashed across the floor, cold and sharp, illuminating the closet door, the dresser, the window,

The window.

A whisper of sound, faint, brittle. Fingernails against glass. A slow, deliberate scrape.

Darren stirred, his eyelids flickering. Another sound. A tap, gentle, patient. The wind? No, the night was still.

His stomach clenched. He turned, pulse hammering, and saw him.

A face, hovering beyond the glass. Pale, hollow-eyed, familiar. Milo. His friend.

But not.

Milo was gone. Had been for days. Buried deep in the earth where the cold seeped in. And yet, there he was, floating just beyond the pane, his mouth stretched into something that might have been a smile, might have been something else. His hands rested against the window, fingers curled slightly, as if they could already feel Darren's skin, already imagine how warm he would be.

Darren couldn't move. Couldn't breathe. A prickling ran down his spine, pooling in his limbs, turning his muscles to stone.

"Darren," Milo whispered. His voice was distant, warped, thick with something rotten. "Let me in."

Darren shook his head. Or tried to. His body was sluggish, heavy, as though something pressed down on him, something unseen, something ancient and patient. A slow, creeping numbness settled in his fingertips, his toes, winding through his veins like ice.

Milo lifted a hand, pressing his palm flat against the glass. His skin looked thin, stretched too tight over the bones, like wax held too close to a flame. His fingernails were long, curling slightly at the tips, yellowed, cracked.

His eyes, His eyes were nothing. Just pits, just hollows where something else looked out.

A low pressure built in Darren's skull, behind his eyes, a silent urging. Open the window. Let him in. Just a little. Just a crack. The latch was so close, barely an arm's length away. His hand twitched, his fingers reaching.

Milo's mouth widened. Not a smile. A cavern, teeth small and sharp and far too many, stretching impossibly. The skin around it strained, split, blackness leaking from the cracks.

Darren whimpered, a sound too small, too useless. His feet were on the floor now, his legs moving without his permission. His fingers, trembling, brushed the latch,

And the night shifted.

A deep, aching groan rippled through the air, the sound of something waking. The shadows in the corners of the room thickened, pulling inward, writhing, reaching. Milo's expression twisted, the gaping mouth snapping shut, his black eyes narrowing in something like frustration. He scratched at the glass, harder now, a frantic, hungry sound.

Darren's breath came in short, ragged gasps. He yanked his hand back, stumbled, fell. The floor was cold beneath him, and for the first time, he felt the full weight of the darkness pressing in, whispering, sighing.

Milo lingered a moment longer, his head tilting in an unnatural jerk, something beneath his skin pushing, shifting, bulging. Milo screamed, a guttural, raw sound, his form twisting, folding, then bursting through the glass with a spray of glittering shards. Darren had no time to react, no breath left to scream, Milo was on him, hands clawing, teeth sinking into his throat. The pain was immediate, hot, wet, but not as terrible as the feeling of something being drawn out of him, siphoned away, leaving an emptiness in its place.

Milo's lips peeled back, blood smeared and glistening, his eyes alight with something beyond hunger, something deeper, darker. Darren gasped, his fingers twitching, reaching for anything, for nothing, as the world blurred, as the shadows closed in, And when they dug up the body to confirm it, the coffin was filled with water. No skin. Just hair. Just teeth. Just Darren's notebook, untouched, floating like a confession no one wanted to read.

Moloch tells him that this is good and to keep writing it, it's going to be made into a movie one day, it'll scare the souls out of people… mmm… souls.

Still in his psychotic cocaine driven writing rampage, the writer continues with input from Moloch. Writing till he has nothing left to give. And then, The final sentence. The last page slid from the typewriter, falling gently onto the growing pile. He just stared at it.

The ink on the page shimmered, as if still wet, then began to move. The letters twisted, untangling from their rigid lines, slithering into grotesque, new configurations. Words that had once belonged to him reformed into something ancient, something unknowable. Sentences curled into spirals, entire paragraphs collapsing in on themselves like dying stars.

Then the pages lifted from the desk, caught in a violent wind that did not exist. Paper whirled around the room, a storm of language tearing itself apart. He gasped as the words latched onto his skin, not resting, but sinking in. Burning. Infesting. His body seized, spine arching back as if a current had shot through him.

His head violently arched back, his mouth tore open, a terrible force wrenched from inside him. The words came screaming out, pouring from his throat and nostrils in a chaotic, howling gale, the taste of ink, the feeling of his throat raw from screaming words he never meant to say. A voice that was no longer his own. They whipped across the room, clawing through the air in a frantic cyclone, before suddenly collapsing inward.

The pages reassembled. One by one, they snapped back into place, stacking neatly as if nothing had happened. And then, the final page, pure, white, untouched, floated downward, drifting like a feather through the still air.

His breath slowed. His pulse thundered in his ears.

As the page landed, ink seeped from the paper's fibres, forming words of its own. It congealed, dark and wet, from the blood of his cocaine-nosebleeds. A title emerged.

"*Bethlehem's Lot.*"

His own, yet never his at all.

This was not fiction. It was a door, a cosmic cipher unlocking something that had been waiting just beyond the veil.

His own handwritten notes sprawled over them like the remnants of a man in decline.

But he had no memory of writing it. His breath caught in his throat.

"The door is open now."

The air thickened. The walls seemed to breathe. The shadows coiled at the edges of his vision. The house creaked like it was exhaling. He slowly looked up from the notepad. Moloch sat across from him on the window seat. Smiling. Pleased. In control.

As his body sagged into the chair, the final rush of adrenaline surged through his veins, the remnants of cocaine burning like liquid fire under his skin. His eyelids fluttered, heavy with exhaustion, and as they drifted shut, Moloch's grin stretched wider, teeth glinting in the dim light. Just before the darkness swallowed him whole, a voice slithered through the void, no longer a whisper, no longer just an idea curling around his thoughts, but audible, real, spoken aloud into the thick, suffocating air.

"Are you having fun yet?"

His eyes snapped open. Involuntary action, the doctors concluded.

He hadn't woken, not really. His body moved on its own, twitches in his fingers, a tightening of the jaw, the faintest flex of his toes under the sheet. A nervous system still firing, even if the mind behind it had checked out. They'd seen it before. Cocaine withdrawals could scramble the brain like eggs if it hit hard enough.

"He's lucky," said one of the doctors, a tall man with permanent frown lines carved between his brows. "Another few hours without intervention, and we'd be talking organ failure."

Martha sat beside the bed, her hands wrung raw, a Styrofoam coffee cup untouched in her lap. "So what now?"

"We taper him down slowly. Fluids, monitored sedation, and a close eye on his vitals. He's going to be in and out, hallucinations, maybe aggression. Could be days before he's properly lucid. We're going to do everything we can, but..." The doctor hesitated, glancing at the readouts. "There's damage. Some of it... may not be reversible."

Martha didn't cry. She just nodded, her jaw clenched like she was holding back a scream too old to sound.

A sudden jerk from the bed made her flinch. His hand spasmed, fingers curling into a fist, then unclenching again like a child grasping at air.

"He might do that," the doctor said gently. "The body sometimes remembers what the mind wants to forget."

The world had shifted.

The room hummed low, machines ticking in quiet rhythm like a dying metronome. Tubes snaked from his arms, from his nose. His skin looked translucent under the hospital light, veins like spiderwebs, bruises blooming violet and yellow at the edges of the tape that held him together.

In the quiet dark of the hospital room, the machines pulsed their slow lullaby of survival.

Miles away, in their home, Grace sat up in bed. Her eyes were wide, her small hands balled into fists against the blanket. The house wasn't asleep, not really. It breathed.

She padded barefoot down the hall, the boards cold beneath her toes. The light under Martha's door spilled out soft and yellow. Grace knocked once, then opened it without waiting.

"Mum."

Martha stirred, eyes heavy. "What is it, sweetheart?"

Grace stood still for a moment. Then: "He's whispering again."

Martha blinked. "What?"

Grace stepped closer. "Daddy. I heard him."

Martha sat up straighter, the sheets sliding off her legs. "He's not even conscious, Grace. He's in a hospital bed."

"I know," Grace said quietly. "But it wasn't with his mouth."

Martha frowned. "What does that mean?"

Grace's eyes welled up. "He's whispering with the air."

Martha froze. For a moment, neither of them moved.

Then something creaked in the walls.

Low. Breathy.

A murmur, indistinct, but not imagined.

The next day Martha sat beside him, cross-legged in the stiff plastic chair, blanket across her knees. One hand resting gently on his, but not holding it. Just enough contact to feel the warmth, to know he hadn't gone entirely cold.

"You look worse now than you did when you left," she whispered. "Even the kids said it. They noticed the dark. It got in you, didn't it?"

No response. Of course not.

"You shouldn't have read *The Shimmering* to them. Not to your friends, not to anyone. That wasn't a story. That was something else."

She leaned forward, her thumb tracing the back of his hand, watching his eyelids for a flicker. Nothing.

"You don't remember what you write anymore, do you?" she asked. "That's the part that scares me most. Because I do."

A pause.

"I remember every line of *Caroline*. Especially the bits you didn't write."

Her voice dropped lower. "You remember when I stayed up after you passed out? When you left it scattered across the living room floor and told me it was finished? It wasn't. You didn't even touch the last thirty pages. Just a loose mess of dialogue and one scene about her hiding in the school bathroom."

She shook her head. Bitter.

"She just hides and cries, like a frightened little lamb. That was it. But I… I wrote the rest. I made her fight back. I gave her the blade. I made her burn that goddamn place down. I made her scream. I made her real. And now you get invited on talk shows for writing 'a raw, feminine horror that captures the secret cruelties between girls.'"

A dry laugh, paper thin.

"That was me, you bastard. I lived that. You were passed out cold, high as a kite, and I was bleeding it onto the page for you."

The machines beeped quietly. His breath shallow. Still no flicker behind the eyes.

Her voice cracked then. Her fingers tightened over his.

"If you come back from this, I'll stay. Just… please don't make me bury you. Not yet."

Another silence, longer this time.

"I can't keep pretending you're getting better. I know you're not. The house knows it. The kids know it. That… *thing* that watches me when I sleep knows it."

She glanced toward the corner of the room. No shadow moved, but her eyes lingered.

"I don't know who you pray to anymore. Maybe you don't. Maybe it's nothing."

She let go of his hand, wiped at her eyes.

"But I do. And if you're still in there, if there's anything left of the man who used to bring me coffee at 5am when I was up with the girls, then hear this."

She stood slowly, leaned down, lips near his ear.

"If you survive this, and you wake up, I'll support you in anything you want to do to get help, I love you to the moon and back."

Her voice fell to a whisper, lower than prayer.

"And if you don't wake up… then, Fuck you."

She turned, stepping away from the bed.

The IV fluid caught the light as it pulsed through the line, still clear, still clean. For now.

But something in the corner of the room shifted. A murmur beneath the machines. A flicker in the vent above.

And Martha didn't see the way the monitor lights dimmed just a fraction. Or the faint smile twitching at the corners of his mouth, not his own. As if something else had heard her promise.

In his mind the world went silent.

Then something peeled open.

A corridor, long, windowless, pulsing gently like something alive. Fluorescent lights above flickered in staccato rhythm, casting shadows that didn't follow the laws of movement. He walked, though his legs didn't move. Each step echoed like thunder on wet tile.

Pages floated in the air around him, thin, yellowed, bleeding ink like oil. They stuck to his arms, wrapped around his legs, slithered up his throat. The ink crawled beneath his skin, turning to veins. Words pulsed inside him.

At the end of the corridor, a door. Plain. White. Waiting like it always had. Always will.

He reached for the knob, but it was warm, like flesh. It opened anyway.

Inside: a room with no walls. Just pages nailed into the dark. Blood writing. Spirals. Latin. Gibberish. All of it whispering backwards.

Martha stood in the middle, her back to him. Her hair damp. Her dress clung to her like she had just stepped from a river.

He tried to speak.

She turned.

But it wasn't her face.

It was his.

Rotting. Grinning. Ink pouring from its mouth.

"You're not the writer," it said. "You're the door."

And then the ceiling peeled open like paper.

And he vacuumed up into the light,

He was no longer in his office, no longer slumped in a chair surrounded by typewritten madness and empty bottles. He was clean. His clothes were fresh, his body weightless, the sharp bite of addiction absent from his bloodstream. The sheets beneath him smelled of detergent, the familiar softness of a bed pressing against his back. Martha sat beside him, her eyes filled with something warm, something real, relief. Love.

"How?" His voice cracked, dry as sandpaper. He tried to sit up, but the pull of an IV in his arm stopped him. "How… when? When did you come back?"

Martha smiled gently, smoothing a hand over his forehead.

"Two weeks ago," she said, her voice soft. "I found you on the floor in a pool of your own, " she hesitated, shaking her head. "Never mind about that. You're okay now. The doctors have been giving you fluids, helping your body recover. You scared me." How long were you gone? A week replied Martha. The Drs say you were lucky I found you when I did.

His throat tightened. "I'm so glad you're back."

"Me too," she whispered. "Me too."

She stood, reaching for the buzzer. "I should call the doctor, let him know you're awake."

Before she could move, he reached out, fingers wrapping gently around her wrist. His grip was weak, but his voice was steady. When she turned back to him, he smiled. "I love you to the moon and back," he said. She covered his hand with hers, squeezing it. "I love you too." But deep in the corners of his mind, where no light could reach, something lingered. Something watched. And it was still waiting. "You think this is recovery?" Moloch whispered. "This is just the intermission." He then looked at the IV drip fluid as it turned black and started to enter his veins.

Chapter 7

Just One More Time

Childhood memories come in shades of white, grey, and black. Some are soft and blurred at the edges. Others, like mine, are sharp, brutal things smothered in violence and abuse, but enough about me. The ones that seem to cause the most trauma are the ones that don't exist at all, wiped clean by something because they're just too dark to face. This was one of those. It was the first time he wrote something that wasn't horror. It had been for Roy. A tribute. A way to let out old emotions and write something different. He had been just four years old when it happened. He remembers leaving the house to go play with Roy, remembers the heat of the sun on his back, the distant hum of cicadas, the way the dust kicked up when they ran. Innocence playing in the morning light, laughter. Then nothing.

The next memory was of coming home, stepping through the front door, his hands dirty, his face pale. But the strangest part, he didn't say a word. He just stood there in the entryway, silent, frozen, his tiny body unable to process whatever had just happened.

His mother crouched down, called his name, but he only blinked at her. His throat locked tight.

It wasn't until much later that he learned the truth.

Roy was dead. Struck by a train.

His family had told him, speaking in hushed tones, watching his face carefully, but there was no reaction. How could there be? He had no memory of it.

No matter how hard he tried to remember, the tracks, the train, the moment Roy died, there was only blank space. As if someone had reached inside his mind and scooped it out, leaving only the memory of going out to play… and then the static of nothingness until he was back home, mute, unable to explain why.

Even as an adult, even now, he sometimes wonders what his younger self saw, what was so horrific that his own brain had wiped it clean?

And yet, it haunted him all the same. That absence, that hole. The thing he should remember, but doesn't.

It wasn't horror. But it was the first time he had tasted fear, even if he couldn't remember why.

He kept up the daily four-mile walk. Doctor's orders. Reconnect with nature, move the blood, clear the static from his mind. He'd mapped the route out himself: down the old logging road, past the birch stand, then a cut through the tree line toward Lake Cezar. It was quiet out there, the kind of quiet that didn't feel forced. No TV, no ringing phones, no ticking clocks. Just the soft crunch of his boots against the dirt and the occasional snap of a twig behind him that he always told himself was a squirrel.

Near the edge of the lake, he stepped behind a tree to take a piss, shook three times (any more and you're wanking, his mind told him, giving himself a small chuckle), zipped up, and wandered into the clearing. The sun caught the water in long gold streaks, clouds drifting low like they couldn't be bothered climbing any higher. Blueberries clung to the edge of the field, tucked low in the scrub. He crouched and picked at them idly, one eye on the shoreline, the other on his watch. He'd have to head back soon. Martha liked to know where he was these days. Part of the recovery process, the therapist had said.

A breeze rolled in from across the water, soft and cool. It brushed past him like a memory. For a moment, he let his eyes close, just breathing, just being. It felt almost okay. Like maybe this, this field, this walk, this hour of quiet, was enough.

Then, faint as smoke on the wind, he heard it.

It's to protect you.

He froze. Not afraid. Just… unsure. It could've been anything. Wind through the grass. Leaves shifting. An old phrase from a dream. He looked around, saw no one.

But something about it stuck like peanut butter to the top of his mouth.

He waited, listening for it again, but the voice never returned. Just silence. Just the soft sounds of the lake and the weight of everything he couldn't quite name pressing in from all sides. He told himself it was nothing. A trick of exhaustion. An echo from inside. But the feeling lingered, that someone, or something, had whispered something to him. And worse, he didn't quite catch it.

He left the lakeside slower than he arrived, the sound of the voice still ringing like a dream he couldn't shake. His boots crunched the gravel path in steady rhythm, each step carrying him closer to the house and further from whatever peace the lake had offered.

Halfway through the trees, another sound rose up behind his eyes, not wind, not birdsong, but Martha's voice, curling out of memory.

"You've got your meeting."

He'd been standing in the office doorway at the time, fingers still tingling from the typewriter. The draft was only half there, the story not yet a story, but something raw and bleeding.

"I'm fine," he'd said, not turning around.

Her voice again, gentler this time. "Please."

That part stuck.

Not the command. Not the concern. Just the softness of it. Like she was asking him not to vanish completely.

He'd followed her out to the car without a word. He remembered the sound of her keys, the way she checked his seatbelt without thinking. Like she was buckling in a ghost.

Martha had sat in the car, engine off, watching through the fogged windscreen as he disappeared down the concrete steps into the church basement. She didn't follow. Not because she didn't care, but because she did, and caring had begun to feel like trespassing.

She remembered simpler times. When addiction meant a hangover and not a haunting. When he used to read her the first pages of everything, drunk with excitement and not whiskey. When writing was just a need, not a hunger.

When their kids didn't flinch at his shadow.

Now, she dropped him at meetings and waited like a parole officer. She hated this version of herself. The silent passenger. The careful warden.

She sighed, twisting her wedding ring out of habit, and looked out at the wet gravel.

Inside the basement, the chairs were already circled. Fluorescents hummed overhead, casting everyone in the shade of dying moths. He took a seat at the back. Didn't give his name. Didn't say a word.

The man leading the session, Denim Jacket, late fifties, swollen knuckles, was halfway through a story about crashing his car into his ex-wife's mailbox three Christmases in a row before he found God in detox.

A few heads nodded.

He didn't.

Then the old man arrived.

Nobody saw him come in. One second, the chair in the far corner was empty. The next, it wasn't. The man sat with his legs crossed, a wool coat draped over his knees despite the summer heat, a cane resting against his thigh. His face looked like it had been carved from driftwood and dried in the sun. Grey, cracked, unreadable.

His eyes locked onto the writer instantly.

"Not your name," the old man said. His voice was barely above a whisper, but it cut across the room like a scream. "Not your skin either. You wear it like a borrowed coat."

Everyone turned. Silence thickened.

"You've got something in you," he continued. "I see it. I smell it."

He'd frozen. His heart pounded. Every nerve had said leave now, but he couldn't move.

The old man's head tilted. "You can tell it I said hello." He smiled then. Empty gums. "Tell it Baal remembers." He paused, then added almost absently, like it was a joke no one else got: "It always says the same thing, you know. Just one more time."

Then he'd leaned back in his chair and said nothing else for the rest of the meeting.

Martha had looked down at her watch. Forty-five minutes. She'd wiped condensation from the glass with her sleeve and waited. She'd wait a lifetime if she had to. That's what you do when someone you love turns into someone else.

Ten minutes later, he'd emerged, a little paler than when he went in, eyes wide and searching the lot like something might follow.

When he opened the passenger door, she asked gently, "How'd it go?"

He'd shrugged. "Waste of time."

She hadn't answered.

As she started the engine and pulled away, she'd glanced at him again, just briefly. He looked like he hadn't blinked in a while.

His hand trembled in his lap.

And far behind them, in the glowing windows of the church basement, the old man had sat alone now, smiling with his eyes shut, mouthing something only the shadows could hear.

The memory faded as the trees broke open and the house came into view. By the time he reached the door, the sun was burning low in the evening sky. He didn't speak. Didn't eat. Just walked straight to the office.

There was something he needed to do.

A story to finish.

A feeling to bury.

Writing this novella caused so many emotions to surface that he wasn't prepared to face. He's been clean for a few months now since his major collapse. Since that night Martha found him. He's been questioning how to manage sobriety. What won't allow his mind to remember what happened to Roy? Did he have a role to play in his death? Guilt at not being able to stop it? Why is this memory gone? And what did that lake whisper?

The story he wrote for Roy was now complete. Satisfied that it gave him the cathartic release he desperately needed. He had already titled it *"The Boy"*.

Then he leaned back in his chair, eyes scanning the desk, heart trying to be still. It's then that he saw it. A piece of paper with a line written in red marker, something he doesn't recall writing, sending a chill through him "Just one more time" is all it said but as a junkie he knew exactly what it meant. Sitting there he traced the edges of the desk with his fingertips, heart hammering, knowing exactly where it was but pretending he didn't. Just for a moment. Just to prove to himself that he was still in control. But he wasn't. He never was. The idea percolated in his mind until it got the better of him. Taped to the underside of the third drawer on his right, just where he left it, was the satchel of cocaine. The one Martha never found. The one that had been waiting for him. His "emergency stash". The burn seared through his sinuses, electric and bitter. His body knew this feeling. His hands stopped shaking, his breathing slowed. A familiar numbness settled over him, and for the first time in months, he didn't feel like himself. He felt like nothing at all. the light danced across the desk and then. Darkness. He's in an abyss of emptiness where the stars look like he's seeing them through a veil.

And then, like a fuse snapping in his mind, the numbness cracked open into heat and colour.

He was four years old.

The sun overhead boiled white in the sky, bleaching everything to bone. He stood near the tracks, barefoot, a stick in one hand, the other shielding his eyes. Dust swirled around his ankles. Cicadas screamed.

Roy was there. Laughing. Running up and down the gravel slope, arms spread like wings, yelling something the wind shredded before it reached him.

Then silence.

Not the silence of thought, but something colder. Manufactured.

He turned.

Something moved beside the rails.

It crawled, no, slithered, no, stumbled forward like a puppet without strings. Arms. Legs. More arms. Wet, black limbs unfolding from beneath a torn yellow sheet. Where a face should have been, there was only paper. Scribbled lines. Spirals. Ink.

And it was looking at him.

The world shook. The sky collapsed into static. Roy screamed, but not like a boy. Not anymore.

Then,

Snap.

Back in the present. His head jerked sideways, smacking against the desk leg. His nose began to bleed again, hot, immediate, tasting of rust and something else.

He didn't move.

Didn't wipe the blood away.

Because for just a second, the memory had been real. The sun. The scream. The thing under the sheet.

And in his mind, still echoing behind the static:

"You saw it too."

Martha came home from doing chores in town and, while putting the groceries away, it dawned on her, there was no sound in the house. No typewriter clacking away, and his new Apple II, which looked like it belonged in a NASA control room, was just as loud. But nothing. Silence. He was home; the de Ville was in the driveway.

She called out his name. No answer. She stepped into the office, expecting to see him slumped at the typewriter, maybe asleep, maybe just lost in thought. But the chair was empty.

A strange, creeping dread slid up her spine. Something felt off. The silence crept in like a ghost, soft and unwanted. She went outside to check the garden. Nothing.

Panic started to rise. He knew he was supposed to tell her, or at least leave a note, if he stepped out. Especially now. Especially with everything. She picked up the phone and called Bud's bar to see if he'd relapsed. Bud swore, hand on heart, he hadn't seen him in months. Said he was kinda glad, the drinking had gotten out of control. Then, with a dry chuckle, added he missed the income. I bet she said, thanks, then she hung up the phone on the receiver.

Martha took a deep breath and focused on a positive outcome, he's just forgot to say where he was going that's all, he'll be back from a walk soon and we'll both have a chuckle over it. She grabbed a few reams of paper she'd picked up from Sears. It's when she went behind the desk to put them away, she saw him.

He was slumped down under the desk, she didn't see him the first time because the light hit the room just right where the sun beam crossed right in front of his body. He wasn't breathing. Martha couldn't find a pulse and he was unresponsive. With lightning speed, the kind that only a superhuman mother could pull off she reached up to the phone and called 911.

911 Call Transcript – July 10, 1982

- -

911 Operator: 911, what's your emergency?

Martha: (breathless, shaky) My husband, he's on the floor. He's not moving. I can't, I can't find a pulse.

911 Operator: Okay, ma'am, my name is Catherine. What's your name?

Martha: (swallows hard, voice cracking) Martha. My name's Martha.

Catherine: Alright, Martha, I'm here with you. I need you to stay as calm as you can, okay?

Catherine: Okay, Martha, What's your address?

Martha: 39 West Broadway

Catherine: Martha, stay with me help is on the way. Can you tell me, is he breathing?

Martha: (frantic rustling, muffled whimpering) I, I don't know. He's under the desk. He's too big, I can't pull him out. I can't, (a frustrated sob, hands slapping against wood as she tries again to move him)

Catherine: I understand, Martha. I need you to look closely. Can you see his chest rising? Hear anything?

Martha: (panting, voice rising) I don't, I don't think so. His face is blue. Oh God, he's blue. Catherine, please,

Catherine: Okay, Martha, listen to me. You are doing so

good right now. Help is coming fast, but I need you to do something for me. We need to start CPR.

Martha: (voice breaking, shaking her head even though Catherine can't see her) I don't know how, I, I can't,

Catherine: I'll walk you through it, Martha. You can do this. Tilt his head back slightly, pinch his nose, and give two breaths into his mouth. Just two. I'll count with you.

Martha: (small inhale, then she exhales into her husband's mouth, whispering between breaths) Come on, come on,

Catherine: That's it, Martha. Now put your hands in the centre of his chest and press hard. Thirty compressions. Count with me, okay? We'll do this together. If you think you're going to break his ribs you're doing it right.

Martha: (counting between gasps, voice shaking, her hands slamming against his chest, each compression a plea, a prayer, something desperate and raw)

Catherine: You're doing incredible, Martha. Keep going.

Martha: (crying, her voice barely holding together) Why isn't he waking up?

Catherine: The paramedics are almost there, Martha. You are not alone. Keep going. Just keep going.

Martha: (voice cracking into something broken, whispering to her husband now) Don't you dare do this to me. Not like this. Not now.

Catherine: Martha, you with me? Do you know if he's taken anything?.

Martha: (Hesitant but resolute to help) He's a recovering junkie, cocaine and other substances, I couldn't tell you really, he's been clean for months.

[Distant sound of sirens approaching]

Catherine: Martha, the medics are pulling up now. If you can, go unlock the door. I promise, they'll take it from here.

Martha: (footsteps, door creaks open, a flood of voices, urgent, professional, commanding. A sob escapes her, somewhere between relief and terror.)

Catherine: Martha, they're going to take care of your

husband. And they're going to take care of you too. Can you put one of them on the phone for me?

[Muffled sounds as phone is handed over, a new voice comes on, steady, no-nonsense, clipped with experience.]

Medic: This is Peter. Who am I speaking with?

Catherine: Peter, this is 911 dispatch, Catherine speaking. The wife has performed CPR, no confirmed pulse before EMS arrival. Likely substance-related. Please confirm transport status as soon as possible.

Peter: Understood. We'll assess and radio in once we're en route.

[The call ends abruptly. The phone clicks dead.]

Peter turns to Martha, his tone shifting, professional but with a hint of warmth. "Martha, I'm Peter. We're going to take care of your husband. Do you know what he took?"

Martha shakes her head, eyes darting between her husband's still body and the team working around him. "No, I don't know. But… he's a recovering alcoholic. Cocaine too. He's been clean for months."

Peter exchanges a quick look with another medic. "The nosebleed might indicate a relapse. We'll check for any other injuries. Do you have a preference for which hospital?"

Martha exhales sharply, pressing her fingers against her lips. "No. Just, just get him there. Please."

The team moves fast. They check his vitals, searching for any additional signs of trauma, lifting his heavy frame onto the stretcher with the kind of precision that only comes from too much practice. The wheels of the gurney squeak as they manoeuvre through the hallway, Martha trailing behind them, arms wrapped around herself.

Then, a groan. Weak, hoarse, but a sound.

Martha stops in her tracks, her breath catching. One of the medics leans in, checking his airway, adjusting his position slightly. "That's good," Peter murmurs, nodding to himself. "He's responding to the movement."

Martha wipes at her eyes. "That means he's going to be okay, right?"

Peter doesn't answer that. "It means he has a shot. A long shot, but a shot nonetheless"

They load him into the back of the ambulance, starting an IV line, running oxygen, stabilizing what they can. The doors slam shut, the sirens wail, and they race off toward Maine General.

The interior of the ambulance pulsed with unnatural light. Red. White. Red. White. His mind flickered in time with it, like an old film reel on the verge of snapping. Every breath rasped through the oxygen mask, a tunnel of cold plastic and gasps.

Peter's voice came in muffled and wrong, wet cotton stuffed in his ears. Words didn't matter, only cadence. The calm tone of someone used to death.

"BP's dropping."

"Push five more."

"Hang on, mate. Just hang on."

Static burst behind his eyes. Then something moved in the mask. A reflection? No. A shadow beneath the plastic, curling and twitching at the edge of his periphery. It grinned. Teeth sharp as typewriter keys. Moloch.

"You always crawl back, don't you?" the reflection whispered.

He tried to speak, to scream, but no sound came. Only fog on the mask.

Then the gurney across from him. He hadn't noticed it before. Or it hadn't been there.

Roy.

Four years old, knees scabbed, eyes wide open. Dead eyes. A child's body zipped to the chest in a stained yellow sheet, arms stiff at his sides. But the mouth moved.

"You left me."

His stomach lurched. Veins writhed like snakes under his skin.

Roy's voice again, lower now, like something else had borrowed it.

"You remember now, don't you?"

A sudden jolt of the ambulance, reality crashed back in with the squeal of rubber and steel. He blinked, breath heaving behind the mask. The gurney across from him was empty. Just straps and a folded sheet.

Peter leaned in. Adjusted something near the IV. "Stay with me," he muttered, almost to himself.

But the whisper was still there, under the roar of tyres and sirens.

Just one more time.

Martha stands in the driveway for a moment, the afternoon air pressing in, watching the red and white lights streak into the distance. Then she turns and moves inside. There's nothing left to do now but follow.

In the hospital while in his weakened state, he sees Moloch fully for the first time since he sat across from the dining table, a figure of impossible darkness, standing at the edge of his vision, watching, waiting. The doctor tells him that if he does not stop, he will not survive. But before he dissipates into a mist Moloch leans in and whispers: We've got work to do, you and I.

"He needs to spend a few nights at the hospital to come down safely," the doctor told Martha.

"Yes. Of course," she replied.

"We'll keep an eye on him. But this can't continue. He can't keep going like this."

She turned to the hospital window. Rain tapped the glass. Somewhere behind the sterile lights and measured breaths, she could feel it again, that awful stillness, like something was waiting for him to wake up. Or worse, already had entered his mind while he's been out of it.

Martha stayed by the bed long after the doctor left. The rain had long since stopped. The only sound now was the hush of the machines and the distant rattle of a trolley in the corridor. She sat still, watching the rise and fall of his chest, counting each breath like it might be the last.

She reached into her coat pocket and pulled out a folded piece of paper. It was old, yellowing at the edges, creased so many times it was barely holding together. A story he wrote. One of the first. Back when it was still fun. When he'd leave her pages on the kitchen bench like love letters. She read the first line again, lips moving with it, but no sound.

Her eyes stung.

She leaned forward, placed the paper gently on the bedside table, and smoothed it flat.

"I miss him," she said, softly. "The man who wrote that. The man who used to kiss me behind the supermarket when we were too poor to eat out."

She wiped her face with her sleeve, then took his hand in both of hers.

"I don't care about the books. Or the tours. Or any of it."

Her voice broke.

"I just want my friend back."

She stayed there in silence, forehead resting lightly against his knuckles, until the machines sang their lullaby again and the sky outside turned a gentler shade of grey.

Chapter 8

Kristina

The hospital lights buzzed low above his bed, fluorescent hum folded into the sterile quiet of the ward. The rain tapped lightly at the window as if it, too, didn't want to wake him. His wrist was tethered to an IV, heart monitored by a steady, slow rhythm. Beep-beep. Beep-beep.

Martha sat beside him, chin in her palm, her paperback opened in her lap. A copy of "Midnight's Children" by Salman Rushdie. She'd been reading the same sentence for an hour. Maybe longer. Who knows really. A nurse moved past the door and paused just briefly to check his chart. "Rapid eye movement. He's dreaming," she murmured. Martha didn't look up. "He does that a lot now." "That's good," the nurse lied, then walked off in a calculated controlled stroll to the next room while looking at her charts.

In the dream, the sky was melting. The sunset over the gravel carpark stretched in a bruised peach haze. Crickets chirped in lazy rhythm. The de Ville was nowhere. The hospital was gone. And there it was again, that car. Red and white. Chrome trim glinting like a grin. A 1958 Plymouth Fury, parked on the same dirt lot it had been all those years ago, its long fins and slick lines cleaner than memory allowed. Donald Johnson leaned against the hood, cigarette in one hand, a fading smile on his face. The back brace still hugged his frame. "Yeah, she's mine," he said, same as before. "But she's temperamental. Bit like a jealous girlfriend when you spot a younger model, ha ha, you know what I mean?" The car engine growled under the hood like it was laughing. The headlights blinked awake. And then the lot blurred. The years folded in on themselves. Barney was there now. Greased hair. Leather jacket. Acne gone. Eyes hard.

Kristina purred in the garage. Beth choked in the passenger seat. The odometer ticked backwards. Johnson's daughter screaming. Suicide in the front seat. Blood misting the windshield. Kristina circling the junkyard like a dog scenting revenge. Daniel. Beth. The final showdown. Barney's spine snapping as he tried to push her. Beth running. Daniel watching. Kristina waiting. And then he was back at the house. His childhood home. The driveway dark, the front porch light buzzing. The Plymouth parked there like it belonged. The front door opened. A boy stepped out. Four years old. Stick in one hand. Dust around his ankles. He looked up at the car. He didn't smile.

His body lurched in the hospital bed. The machines spiked. Martha stood instantly. "It's okay. You're okay," she whispered. His mouth moved like he wanted to speak. Nothing came out. A nurse came in, adjusted the IV. "Welcome back." He turned his head slowly toward Martha. "Can I have a pen?" She blinked. "Now?" "Please."

He couldn't write as he was too tired, so he dictated the dream to Martha who did her best to write it all down as he blurted it all out before it was gone.

His voice cracked halfway through. Hands trembling, eyes glazed. Martha wrote like a stenographer in court, barely keeping up, terrified the thread would snap.

You remembered all that?" she asked, eyes wide.

"No," he said. "But it remembered me."

The doctor came in the next morning, clipboard in hand, expression carved from stone.

Martha stood at the window, arms folded, watching the rain.

"You shouldn't have survived this," he said, not unkindly. "That amount in your system, combined with your history, frankly, it's a miracle."

He didn't answer. Couldn't. His throat still felt like sandpaper, mouth dry from oxygen. But he met the doctor's eyes.

"This wasn't just a lapse," the doctor continued. "This was a suicide attempt, whether you meant it to be or not."

Martha flinched, just slightly.

The doctor sighed. "You're not invincible. Your body's showing signs of long-term damage. If you keep this up, there won't be a next time."

Still, he didn't speak.

"You want to write?" the doctor said, voice low now, just for him. "Write. But understand something, you don't get many more pages unless you stop killing the author."

He left without waiting for a response.

Martha stayed at the window a long time. Neither of them said anything. Not then.

But that night, when he asked for the legal pad again, she handed it to him in silence. Not in approval. Not in surrender. Just love, exhausted and quiet.

He began writing before the room even went dark.

Back home, he moved slower. Still sore. Still drifting. He slept in small doses, ate because Martha reminded him to. The TV played background noise to a room neither of them occupied. Fan mail piled up unopened on the hall table. The garden grew wild. And the typewriter, once the altar he knelt before, stayed cold. Lifeless.

Instead, he took to the legal pad. Spiral-bound, coffee-stained, pages yellowed at the edges. He curled into the armchair by the window with it and a pen from the kitchen drawer. He didn't think. Just wrote. Words bled from somewhere beneath the gauze in his brain. Not a story, not yet, more like pieces of something broken he was trying to lay out in the sun. Scribbled names, questions, jagged phrases circling the same thought: Kristina, a possessed car. Barney. Beth. Daniel. Don't forget the daughter. Spirals in the glass. Grease in his hair. The odometer ran backwards. It always says the same thing.

It came fast and clean. No panic. No fear. Just clarity. Like it had been waiting.

A draft began to form. First paragraph. Then another. The scratching of pen to paper became its own kind of breathing.

Martha stopped in the doorway with a mug of tea, wearing his hoodie. Her voice was quiet. "Kristina?" He looked up. "It's just a story." She stepped in, glanced at the pad. "Just don't let it become more than that." He nodded. But his eyes never left the page. His fingers cramped white against the spiral. He didn't stretch them. Didn't stop.

Because something inside had clicked.

He stayed in the chair long after the sun dipped, writing by lamplight, hand shaking, but steady.

Barney changed as the car was rebuilt. Just like he had. Glasses vanished. Pimples faded. Kindness eroded. Beth was no one, and then she was everything. Grief in a girl's shape. He wrote the choke scene. Beth gasping, clawing the air. Kristina's dashboard glowing, unblinking. The glovebox, too. Where Donald Johnson's spirit curled tight into the lining, fused with static and old receipts. Barney dressing in dead men's clothes, talking like the past never ended. Kristina dragging time backwards, spinning it like a tape. Obsession. Identity. Violence. Hunger.

He wasn't inventing anything. He was confessing.

And when he put the pen down, he realised the ache in his chest had a name. Roy.

Still trying to make sense of it. Still looking for a shape that fit.

Kristina wasn't a metaphor. Not really. She was a mirror. And he'd been afraid to look.

He flipped the pad to the front. Wrote the title clean in block letters. Kristina. Then sat back and watched the page settle.

From the hallway: the sound of Martha washing up. Kids' laughter on the TV. A spoon in a mug. Life hadn't stopped. Not yet.

But this story would cost him something. Maybe it already had.

Martha watched from the kitchen one night. He stood in the driveway, barefoot, arms limp, staring at the gravel like something ought to be parked there. She stepped outside. The porch light caught him like a memory. "You okay?" He jumped. "Just getting air." She joined him. "Don't go back," she said. He nodded. Almost like it was still a choice. They stood together, silent. She leaned gently into his shoulder. "Sometimes I feel like I've already left," he said. "Like I'm watching it all happen from somewhere else." "You're here now. Don't give that up. Not for her. Not for any story." He closed his eyes. The night too big. The space too empty. But he whispered, "Okay." And meant it, if only for the moment.

Weeks passed. He kept his head down, took his walks, made every meeting he could stomach. Martha brought coffee and Like before, she read what he wrote. Suggested cuts. Trimmed the fat. Made it real.

The story arrived sharp, clear, precise. Like it had waited for him to catch it.

He wrote Beth choking. The headlights glowing green. Donald Johnson, small and seething in the glovebox. Barney in someone else's life. Kristina spinning the past.

Then, late on a Tuesday, he finished. Thunder rolled beyond the hills.

He slid the final page from the typewriter. Held it. Coffee-stained. Dog-eared. Alive.

Kristina.

It stared up at him.

Outside, the rain began. Inside, he finally exhaled. Not with fear. Not with dread. With something else.

Like maybe this one, just this once, had been enough

But the next day, he walked.

The air carried that strange in-between stillness, like the world was holding its breath. Clouds hung low and heavy, the kind that didn't promise rain, just pressure. The gravel shifted under his boots with each step, too familiar now to even register. His body moved on instinct. The mind was elsewhere.

Four miles. Same as always. Through the birch stand, across the break in the tree line, down toward the water.

He didn't come for the exercise anymore. That part had long stopped being true.

It was the voice.

That flicker of sound he'd heard by the lake, the first time, months ago now, though it never stopped echoing.

It's to protect you.

Or something like that.

He was never sure. It came like breath caught in a dream, half-heard, half-remembered, maddening in its kindness. Because it didn't feel like a warning. It felt like shelter. Something had him. Despite everything.

Despite the relapse. Despite the lies he told Martha and himself. Despite the shadow in his veins, whispering in Moloch's tone, work to do, work to do.

Whatever the voice was, it didn't want anything from him.

It had simply spoken.

And that was enough to keep him coming back. Day after day. Same walk. Same route. Same stretch of rock overlooking Lake Cezar.

He stood there again now, boots planted firm, eyes scanning the still water. He closed them. Listened.

The wind pressed gently at his back. The lake lapped against the shore in quiet repetition. His heart thudded once, then again.

No voice.

Not today.

"Please," he whispered, barely audible. "I just want to know what you said."

He didn't ask for more. Just clarity. Just to know that he'd heard it right. That the line he'd clung to like a rope, It's to protect you, had meant what he hoped it did.

That he hadn't imagined it. That he hadn't broken so far that kindness now sounded like hallucination.

He opened his eyes slowly. Nothing had changed.

But he didn't leave. Not yet. He stood there as the sun dipped low behind the trees and the air turned sharp. It didn't matter that the voice never came. That the message remained blurred at the edges.

What mattered was that something once saw him and didn't flinch. It saw the addict, the coward, the liar, and didn't run.

It tried to protect him.

So he'd keep walking. Keep showing up. Keep listening.

Because whatever it was, it wasn't Moloch.

And that meant, maybe, there was still something out there worth believing in.

A black feather floated past his feet, slow and lazy in the breeze.

He didn't see it as he turned to go back to the house. Maybe tomorrow he said to himself. Maybe tomorrow.

Back at his desk, fingers twitching over the keyboard, the hum of his own mind too loud, too intrusive. He hadn't touched a drink in three weeks, not since the overdose. His hands still ached for the weight of a glass, still remembered the burn of whiskey tracing fire down his throat, filling the cracks inside him. But something had shifted in the way he approached the bottle now. It wasn't willpower keeping him from drinking. It wasn't discipline.

It simply didn't matter anymore.

The decision had been made, though he wasn't sure whether it had been his or something that had been placed inside him. The urge was still there, coiled deep in the recesses of his mind, but it was no longer a struggle. The whiskey sat on the counter, untouched, the dust forming around its base. He had thought once that overcoming addiction would be a victory, a sign of strength, but there was no sense of triumph in this. It was just another thing that had been taken from him, another part of himself lost in the slow corrosion of his identity.

Instead, he sat there, staring at the manuscript.

The title flickered on the screen, *The Offering*. He hadn't called it that. His pulse stuttered. The pages quivered. He blinked once. And the letters shifted. Then they moved. His hallucinations are becoming more frequent despite being clean.

Ink spilled from the page, stretching, twisting, curling into long, black legs. A thousand tiny spiders birthed from the words, crawling across his desk, spilling onto his arms, his skin, his throat, millions of them, writhing, digging into his flesh, their tiny limbs scuttling across the surface of his body, burrowing into the crevices of his skin.

His scream tore through the silence as they poured into his mouth, forced their way down his throat, filled his lungs with suffocating, writhing bodies. They crawled up behind his eyes, burrowing deep into the soft tissue of his mind, their bites gnawing at the foundation of his sanity. He clawed at his face, his arms, his skin peeling beneath his fingernails, but no matter how much he tore at himself, they kept coming. Each bite festered, flesh rotting away, decay spreading outward in pulsing waves, turning him into something unrecognizable, something hollow.

The skittering filled his skull. Scratching. Gnawing. Rewriting.

His screams filled the room, his fingers scraping against the desk, knocking over the bottle of ink, watching as it bled across the floor in a pool of darkness that pulsed and shifted with skittering legs.

Then,

A voice, smooth, laughing, curling through the room like smoke slipping beneath a locked door, its presence settling into the space between his breaths.

"Afraid, are we?"

And just like that,

The spiders were gone. The ink was dry. Moloch was reasserting his grip.

His breath came in ragged gasps, his heart slamming against his ribs, sweat dripping from his forehead onto the paper. The words had changed again. His gaze darted to the whiskey bottle. It was already empty. He swallowed hard, the weight of the hallucination pressing down on him, reality bending and snapping like an overstretched wire.

This is crazy. The blend of reality and delusion was becoming unbearable.

From exhaustion and drinking a whole bottle of whisky he passed out at his desk. Martha, walked in after it was too late. Shit. I knew I should have emptied that bottle in the sink. Knowing there wasn't anything she could do right now she got a blanket and lovingly wrapped it over him. She ran her hands through his hair, whispered in his ear that he's safe and that she's got his back. She told him she loved him kissed his forehead and went back to the kids in the living room.

The next evening, Martha made a comment about Grace's unusual silence. She sat at the dinner table, head down, pushing food around her plate, her movements slow, almost methodical.

Alex had a bruise on his wrist, half-hidden beneath his sleeve. The author's stomach twisted.

"Who?" he asked.

Neither of them answered.

He had been bullied once. Beaten, spat on, forgotten, and he would not let it happen to them. The next day, he found them waiting behind the schoolyard, a pack of little shits, laughing, shoving, testing the boundaries of cruelty, their taunts sharp as knives. The moment the author stepped forward, the air changed. The laughter died, the weight of something unseen pressing against them, pulling at the edges of their instincts. The ringleader, a sneering boy with dead, glassy eyes, stood his ground, but the others shuffled back.

Moloch stirred.

It was not a decision.

It was instinct.

The author's shadow stretched unnaturally, bending toward the boy like something with a mind of its own. The boy's mouth twisted open, silent at first, lips stretched in a soundless scream before his body convulsed. His eyes rolled back, his limbs twitching as something unspoken broke inside him. And then, in a way both slow and instant, Moloch stepped inside.

The other children ran.

The boy's body jerked, muscles locking as his fingers curled into claws, his mind twisting, reshaping, fracturing under the pressure of something too vast, too incomprehensible. The author felt it, the break. The snap of something delicate, something irreplaceable. And then, just as suddenly as he had entered, Moloch stepped back, leaving the boy empty. His body collapsed onto the pavement, mouth still twitching, drool running down his chin. His eyes were vacant, his soul scrambled beyond recognition.

Moloch turned to the author and nodded. Like it had been a favour. Like it was something owed.

The author stumbled back, breath ragged, skin clammy with sweat.

He stumbled away from the schoolyard like a man fleeing the scene of a crime, because that's what it was, wasn't it? A crime. Not one the law would recognise, but something deeper. A violation older than language.

His legs moved without instruction, carrying him two streets down and into the narrow choke of an alley behind an abandoned shopfront. The stink of sour milk and bin juice hit him just as his stomach revolted. He doubled over behind the rusting skip and threw up, everything, nothing, bile and dread, the last of his control.

It splashed hot against the concrete. Strings of saliva clung to his lips. He wiped them with the back of his sleeve, breath heaving, eyes stinging.

"I didn't ask for this," he said.

His voice barely rose above a whisper. But the alley heard him. The bricks, the bins, the sky.

And then,

"Didn't you?"

The voice came not as a whisper, not as breath.

It cracked through the alley like thunder from inside his chest.

He flinched. Not from fear. From truth.

Because he had.

Of course he had.

The room was small, the walls the colour of old milk, peeling near the edges where nervous hands had picked at them. The window overlooked a patch of dead grass and a parking lot where visitors came and went, their lives continuing, unaffected, unaware of the broken thing inside. He sat by the window, rocking, sucking his thumb, mind vacant, drifting somewhere unreachable.

He didn't scream at night. Didn't cry. Didn't talk. Didn't do much of anything at all. But one day, he tried.

The therapist, a woman with tired eyes and a gentle voice, leaned forward in her chair, notebook balanced on her lap.

"Go on, Tommy. You can tell me."

The boy's eyes shifted, something flickering behind them, the barest whisper of memory struggling to surface. His lips parted, breath shallow, tremulous, words balancing on the edge of existence. He wasn't looking at her anymore. He wasn't looking at anything in the room.

He was looking at the shadow in the corner.

The lights flickered.

The room chilled.

Moloch stepped forward, unseen by her. Unseen by anyone but him.

A grin. A giggle. A cold pressure sliding into his chest like a hand pressing against his lungs. The boy whimpered, shoulders curling inward as his breath hitched.

The therapist frowned. "It's okay, Tommy. You're safe here."

He wasn't.

A sudden, violent slap against the back of his head.

His body jerked.

His eyes rolled back.

His limbs twisted.

The fragile, flickering moment of clarity vanished.

The therapist reached forward, her voice suddenly far away. "Tommy?"

The boy's hands slowly unclenched. The air felt thick, too still, the window dimming as if the light itself was withdrawing. A scent lingered, burnt hair, rotting paper, something old and hungry.

The therapist closed her notebook.

"We'll try again tomorrow."

She stood, turning toward the door. Behind her, Tommy's lips twitched. Not into words. Not into anything real. Just a small, involuntary motion.

Almost like a smile.

Chapter 9

Betrayal

The author's fame had grown dramatically since his humble beginnings as a struggling writer all those years ago. Thirty-one bestsellers. Movie deals. TV adaptations. He was a literary god, a junkie god but still a god. Fame was worn like an old favourite cardigan, comfortable, familiar. He wasn't going to win any popularity contests or become a style icon. "He's a nerd writing nerdy books," as one journo had put it.

Looking for something new, his friend Stuart told him about a thing that lived in the sewer grate at the corner of Jackson and Union Street. A local legend, something whispered to eat children. The author got goosebumps. A jolt of electricity in his brain.

He knew, Moloch approved.

The mythical creature had been spotted before, many times before. An enduring shadow over the town's history. The more he excavated, the more it stared back. A revelation occurred: he had to face his own demons. And what terrified him most? Clowns. A form of the monster in the sewer, a grinning, malevolent clown, rummaging the depths behind the scenes for its next victim. But there was more. The folklore of the town spoke of an ancient entity, small but dangerously powerful. A creature known as the Lumpeguin. Was this the same creature he wondered?

Lumpeguin could occasionally be seen frolicking in the waves near the shore… or the sewers as you stepped off the sidewalk into the road grabbing children's legs and dragging them in. Other times it would take pleasure in coercing them to climb down for a party.

Don't let their size fool you though. Their powerful magic made them worthy of respect.

They ate children for fun for fuck sake.

A fitting metaphor. A creature that preyed on the innocent, luring them with laughter and games before dragging them into the abyss. It was his darkest work yet. The prose was raw, visceral, terrifying.

He knew he hadn't written it alone. Though he got high on his own supply sometimes and forgot, Moloch was there, wrapped around his subconscious like a parasite, ensuring the words flowed just right. He craved drugs so much because he was addicted to something worse, Moloch's hunger. And as far as he could tell, the only way he got clarity from Moloch was when he was high. So he hid his hits to when Martha went to bed so she wouldn't know. That's when he'd drink too then finish off with some mouthwash so she couldn't tell. She could always tell.

A few weeks later Martha sat at the kitchen table with the latest manuscript pages spread before her, one hand curled around a chipped mug. They could afford new ones, had for years now, but she insisted on keeping things like this. To remind them they were still human. Just people. She wanted the kids to be normal, as she put it. Grounded, not swallowed by all this madness he wrote and all the madness it brought. These days strangers stood outside their home taking photos doing weird shit, sneaking up the porch to get a glimpse of the King. It got so bad they commissioned a scary as fuck fence out the front with dragons and other creatures to keep the fans happy but too scared to enter at the same time.

Outside, the wind scraped dead leaves against the window. Inside, only the wall clock ticked, slow, deliberate, like it was counting something down. Tick, tick, tick, tick. A rhythm that drove everyone mad but no one said as such so it just stayed, just kept ticking.

She'd promised herself she'd help with the stories. Especially after *Kristina*. Especially after what that one did to him. To her. To all of them.

He'd left the new draft on the table, deliberately or forgetfully, she wasn't sure. But before the kettle even boiled, she found herself flipping through the pages.

The title: *Lumpeguin.*

Ridiculous. Until it wasn't.

The words clawed at her mind. Got under her skin. It was visceral.

It began like folklore. A coastal town. Something small but impossibly ancient. A trickster god in miniature, glimpsed near storm drains or paddling at the surf's edge.

Then: a boy in a yellow slicker. A paper boat. A red grin from the shadows.

She froze. Her tea cooled untouched.

This was him, she realised. This was not far from their street. Jackson and Union. A fictionalised version of the old neighbourhood, rendered with near photographic detail. It wasn't homage. It was excavation.

"You always said you hated clowns," she muttered aloud.

She read on. A band of children, bullied, broken, angry. Silver slugs made from melted coins. The creature changing shape: bird, corpse, phantom. Dread turned into mythology. Absurd, if it wasn't so real. Fear threaded through it. Old, wet fear.

And something darker. Something that hung over every word like mould blooming on damp wallpaper.

He stood barefoot in the doorway behind her, watching her read.

"I didn't think you'd…"

She didn't look up. "This is about you."

He said nothing.

"And them," she added. "Our kids."

Still, silence.

She looked up then. His eyes were red-rimmed. Sleepless. But his hands weren't shaking.

"Is this a new story?" she asked.

"No," he said, then hesitated. "Yes. But I had the idea years ago."

She exhaled slowly. Controlled. "You want me to keep reading?"

His voice cracked, barely a whisper. "Please."

She nodded once. And turned the page.

They said it started back in 1956.

A small town south of Biddeford. No one really remembered its name, but the legends still circled like drain water.

A boy named Jamie had gone missing. Last seen chasing a paper boat down flooded gutters after a storm, it slipped into a sewer grate at the corner of Jackson and Union. He leaned in. Something leaned back. Spoke kindly. Laughed like an uncle. Wore a painted face.

The children called it Buttons.

Buttons the Smiling clown.

Jamie's arm was found weeks later, the bone torn clean.

Then the stories began. A group of kids, outcasts, misfits, half-formed and angry, started whispering about seeing him too. Only he wasn't just a clown anymore. He changed, depending on the child. A dead dog. A mother with no eyes. A soldier rotting in uniform. Something ancient that lived beneath the town, wearing fear like a costume.

The seven kids called themselves The Hollow Seven. They fought it. Or tried to.

One kid, Marlow, swore he saw the real form, a squat creature wrapped in dripping rags, waddling at the sewer's edge with eyes like cigarette burns.

They named it the Lumpeguin.

It laughed as it fed. Didn't hide. Didn't run. Sang when it tore them apart.

Silver could hurt it, the story went. So they forged slugs from a melted coin. And went down into the tunnels.

Most came back.

Not all.

They swore a blood oath to return if it ever came back. But none did. The town dried up. Tracks rusted. Kids moved on. Some committed suicide. One was institutionalised.

No one ever mentioned Lumpeguin again.

Until now.

She turned the page.

It wasn't manuscript anymore. Not prose. Notes. Scribbled margins. Coffee stains. A photocopy of what looked like an old newspaper clipping taped to the sheet with yellowed, curling corners. The ink had bled slightly, like even the pages wanted it forgotten.

Biddeford Gazette, October 1956

LOCAL BOY STILL MISSING AFTER SIX WEEKS – FOUL PLAY SUSPECTED

By Simon Peters

"Jamie Griggs, 7, was last seen on the afternoon of September 14, chasing a paper boat in the storm runoff. Eyewitnesses recall hearing laughter from the sewer grate near Jackson and Union before the boy disappeared from view. 'He was talking to someone,' one neighbour said, 'but no one else was there.' Police have not ruled out the possibility of a kidnapping. A fragment of what appears to be a child's arm was recovered several blocks downstream. A coroner's report is pending."

Underneath it, his handwriting:

THEY SAID THE BODY WAS DRAINED. NO BLOOD. NO BRUISES. NO SIGN OF STRUGGLE. JUST CLEAN BONE AND SOMETHING WRITTEN ON THE GUTTER WALL IN WHAT LOOKED LIKE TAR BUT WAS CONGEALED BLOOD: "FEED US."

Below that, another line. Scrawled in a darker pen.

BUTTONS WAS REAL?

Martha stared. Something cold slid down her spine. She glanced up to find him still standing in the doorway. Watching. Not blinking.

She looked back at the notes. Another margin entry caught her eye:

They never caught what did it because they were never looking in the right direction. Not down.

She stopped reading. Eyes fixed on the next page. But her mind had already pulled away.

"You gave it a voice," she said finally. "The Lumpeguin. That laugh like wet gravel."

He nodded, eyes still on her.

"A mouth that only opens for children. It doesn't just kill… it feasts."

His silence said everything.

"You don't remember writing half of this, do you?"

"It came in flashes," he said. "During blackouts. During the stretches where I wasn't… me."

"Moloch?"

He nodded. Acknowledging him to her for the first time. How did you know?

You've called out to IT when you were in the hospital as she pushed the pages away slightly. Not rejection. Just space.

"It fed on innocence," she said. "On blood. On belief."

"And it still does," he said quietly.

She looked at him then, not with fear, but with something worse.

Pity.

And love.

And fatigue.

"I'll read more tomorrow," she said.

He nodded.

And for the first time in a long time, he let her turn out the light.

'Lumpeguin' dropped like a bomb.

Interviews flooded in. Literary journals called it "a visceral triumph of suburban horror," one reviewer from *The Atlantic* going so far as to say: "This is what King would've written if he'd stopped pulling punches and let the poison run straight to the heart. It's a masterpiece of dread, a modern myth for a generation rotting from within." Another called it "a twisted lens on generational trauma, how the sins we bury in storm drains come back grinning."

There was a televised panel discussion where a critic in a turtleneck called it "a fevered indictment of post-war suburbia, a commentary on the cult of innocence." His co-host, clearly rattled, said, "I couldn't finish it. The scenes with the children… they felt exploitative. Too graphic. Too personal."

Twitter lit up. One thread argued Lumpeguin was a metaphor for parental negligence, each death a punishment for failing to pay attention. Others said it was boring. Rambling. Overhyped. Some called it brilliant and broken in equal measure.

The New Yorker said: 'The book excels at building tension, but buckles under the weight of its own mythology. The ending veers into abstraction, trying to articulate a horror too big to be described, and losing its way in the process'.

Still, it sold. Hundreds of thousands of copies in the first week. The adaptation rights went for seven figures.

But none of that mattered to Martha.

She closed the book after finishing it and didn't speak for hours. Just stared out the window while the kids played on the lawn, laughter muffled by the glass.

When he came in to ask if she was alright, she only said:

"I don't know who you had to become to write that."

And he didn't have an answer.

It won awards. It bought them a new car.

It almost broke her.

But his obsession with Moloch was so pronounced now that he openly talked to him, never in front of people. Never in public, he wasn't stupid. Moloch fed into his fears, into his personal struggles with abuse. Not just of himself, but his inner desire to hurt his own children.

He never really acted on those thoughts. But they haunted him all the same. And that scared him.

He both loved and hated his kids. He's got three now, Grace, Alex, and Philip.

And Moloch? Moloch was the same. The love-hate relationship was building to a crescendo, and the author didn't know how it would end. He's not really sure if he wanted it to end. But the lake has an allure to him, he's seeking out something new, some relief.

He wondered if he would become a victim of a character from his own stories?

Then everything changed in a heartbeat.

He wrote a series of short stories that, to this day, have never seen the light of day. But then, an idea resurfaced, one he'd had years ago. A story about a what he thought was a miserable woman who was a sycophant to a bestselling author, Saul Cooper. It started small. A voice. A scene. A memory he didn't know was his.

He remembered the woman Vale mentioned once. A stranger who'd been at every signing, always at the edge of the crowd, always watching. Not speaking. Her face pale, her smile, her scent. She'd lingered in his dreams sometimes, hands gloved, breath smelling of antiseptic. He built the story around her.

The woman became Fanny Willkie. A fanatical, dangerous nurse who rescues Saul from a car accident after he kills off her favourite character in a series he was famous for writing. She keeps him captive in a secluded cabin, away from anyone, forcing him to rewrite the book to bring her back. Not just the character. The belief. The control.

The words came quickly. Fevered. He wrote like he had a time bomb in his throat. Pages scattered across the house. He ate with ink on his fingers. Slept under a pile of drafts. He didn't notice how real Fanny became, how much of her came from something deeper. From something watching.

Martha found the pages on the floor, scattered like shed skin. She sat at the edge of the bed, reading in silence. Halfway through, she set it down. "You think this is you?" she asked.

He couldn't meet her eyes. "No," he said. "But it's close enough."

He titled the book *'Miserable'* and it was met with wild acclaim. Critics called it his masterpiece. The reviews poured in, haunting, daring, unflinching. But Moloch realised that he was portrayed as Fanny. He wasn't just offended, that'll be an understatement, he was livid. He wasn't a sycophant. He wasn't a muse. He was vindictive, he was a god!. And when he realised what the author had done, what he had turned him into, Moloch manifested. For the first time, he stepped into reality.

It happened the night the book hit *The New York Times* best seller list. A rupture. A force so powerful that reality itself fractured for a moment. A cosmic tantrum. A shockwave tearing through the house. Lightbulbs exploded. The TV combusted. Electrical pulses crackled through the walls. The entire block plus 450 neighbouring homes and businesses, lost power in an instant, it took four days to repair the damage. For a fraction of a second, every shadow in the room stretched toward him, unnatural, moving against the rules of physics. And then, emptiness.

But Moloch wasn't just lashing out. He was going to punish the author in the worst way imaginable. He withdrew completely. Severed the connection. The instant absence of Moloch's presence was like a black hole collapsing in his soul. It wasn't just silence, it was a void so absolute it nearly sent him insane. He felt hollow, his skin crawling, as though something had been peeled out of his flesh, leaving behind nothing but a fragile, cracked shell of a man. It was worse than any withdrawal he had ever known. Worse than cocaine, worse than heroin. This was spiritual heroin. And he had just been cut off.

A week went by. The author unable to function rotted in his own filth. He didn't eat. He didn't sleep. He picked at his skin, convinced something was burrowing underneath it. He tried to write, but the words wouldn't come. He tried to drink, but it didn't help. Nothing helped.

Once, just once, he'd held a kitchen knife to his own throat, stood shaking in the hallway, wondering if death would cut the cord and free him. But he couldn't do it. Couldn't bring himself to find out what waited for him after the end. If Moloch was this cruel in life, what would he be in death? He stood in front of the mirror and talked to nothing, hoping Moloch would hear him. On the seventh day, he was on his knees. Begging. Sobbing.

"Please. Please come back. I didn't mean it. I didn't mean to", And then, a ripple in the glass. The mirror distorted, the reflection shifting out of sync with his own movements. A presence. A pulse. A shape forming behind him in the glass.

Moloch. But distant. Watching from the other side of the mirror, like an entity looking in from another reality.

"Will you betray me again?" Moloch asked.

And like every addict before him, the author lied through his teeth. "Never."

"Say it."

"I will never betray you again."

Moloch stepped forward, emerging from the abyss behind the glass, but he did not enter the author. No. He walked through him. A freezing, suffocating presence passing through flesh and bone, but not absorbing back into him. Instead, he moved into the reflection, he felt every bit of the creature moving through his bones.

The author blinked. His body was his own. But his reflection in the mirror… was not him anymore. The man in the glass stood taller. His eyes were darker. He did not blink when the author blinked. Moloch didn't just return. He owned him completely. Letting him know that he no longer controlled him, he even controlled his own reflection.

And that was the final lesson. Moloch had never been just inside him. Moloch had been around him. And now, he was watching him. Ensuring he never stepped out of line again. Stupefied, the author reached out to touch the mirror, but the reflection didn't respond.

Then, through the glass, Moloch whispered: "I am not just a GOD." "I'm your god."

This declaration from Moloch caused a rare memory to surface, a flashback from childhood, an old Sunday school lesson. The preacher spoke of Moloch, an ancient Canaanite god the Israelites were forbidden to worship. He demanded child sacrifices. A sickening realisation curdled in the author's gut. Is this why I hate my children? Is this why Lumpeguin eats them? Is Moloch asking me to kill?

Not in fiction. Not metaphorically.

For real.

But then, silence. Stillness.

And then something strange. Something calm.

He blinked again and the pressure lifted. No pain. No anxiety. No twitching in the veins or cold sweat on his back. It was all… gone.

He stood upright. Clean. Clear. Centred.

He walked out of the room like nothing had happened.

Later that day, he played with the kids. Kicked the ball around the backyard with Alex. Let Grace paint his fingernails without flinching. Sat with Philip reading *Where the Wild Things Are,* doing the monster voices like he used to.

Even Martha noticed, cocked her head from the hallway, confused, lips parted like she wanted to say something but didn't.

The change was colossal. Overnight.

"Are you okay?" she asked once, softly.

He smiled. Warm. Whole. "I've never felt better."

She wanted to believe it.

And so did the kids. Even though each of them, at separate moments, had paused and stared at him, like something about him didn't quite fit.

But he hugged them. Kissed their foreheads. Told them he loved them. He was father of the year.

They didn't say anything. Just watched him walk away.

Back in the study, the mirror hung on the far wall above his writing desk. Dusty. Unremarkable.

He passed it without looking. Sat down. Picked up the pen.

But the reflection didn't move.

It stayed. Still. Watching. Eyes unblinking.

A fraction too slow. A heartbeat out of sync.

And then, a faint smile.

Chapter 10

Martha

The house had fallen quiet again. Not the haunted kind of quiet that always came after one of his episodes, not the tense silence that wrapped the walls like old gauze. This wasn't dread. This wasn't waiting for the next scream or glass to break or sob to leak through the floorboards. No, this quiet was different. It was chosen. Earned. Like stepping out of someone else's nightmare and drawing your own breath for the first time.

Martha had claimed it.

It wasn't easy. It took years. Decades, maybe. Of keeping the house together, of being the still centre of his chaos. She'd walked barefoot through the storm for so long, she forgot what dry felt like. But now the storm had passed, or maybe just moved upstairs, and she had this. Her corner. Her light.

The wind hissed through the hallway cracks and tickled the curtains in the sunroom, where the only sound was the soft clack of keys. The morning light spilled in thick and gold, pooling around Martha like she was something sacred. She sat at a small desk beside a dying fern and a cold mug of tea, with an old 1910 Underwood typewriter she bought at a flea market for $100 that she sent off to be serviced so it would be ready for her, fingers sitting on the classic keys. The thing was a relic, all clunk and steel, chipped paint and soul. There was something beautiful in its simplicity, in its weight. Just waiting. Ready.

She ran her fingertips across the keys like a pianist finding a tune. Sometimes, she still wondered if it was all pretend, if her words only carried because they followed his shadow. If publishers read her name and saw his. If readers read her stories and heard his voice. A fake writer built on a famous marriage. But she kept typing anyway.

Outside, Grace was helping Alex with his homework on the deck. He was frustrated, he always was with numbers, and she kept telling him it didn't matter, that he'd understand it when he needed to. Their books were spread across a the picnic table, a dog-eared times tables chart flapping gently in the breeze. Inside, Philip sat in the hallway, muttering to himself, drawing monsters in crayon. He had dozens of pages lined up against the wall, each one slightly more abstract than the last. One looked like a rabbit made of teeth. Another was just a woman's face, all eyes.

And her husband?

He was upstairs. Recovering. Again.

She'd found him on the bathroom floor again last night, curled around the toilet, whispering apologies to no one. The whisky bottle had been half-empty when she went to bed, completely gone when she got up. The air still smelled like sweat and regret. She hadn't said anything, just pulled a blanket over him and left a glass of water by the sink. Maybe he was writing now. Maybe not. Maybe he was trying. Maybe he was just staring at the wall. She no longer cared to guess. There was a time when she did, when she tried to fix it. That time was over.

Her manuscript was now sitting at fifty-seven thousand words. And for the first time, they were hers. All hers.

It had started as a distraction from his chaos. Something to do when the mirror whispered. When he tossed in his sleep and mumbled names of characters that didn't exist. When the house grew heavy with the wet rot of horror fiction. She'd spent decades editing his work, pruning his madness into publishable form. Proofing stories that made her teeth itch. She'd found the rhythm in his chaos. Learned how to anticipate the spirals, soften the sharpest edges, slip in clarity like thread through a needle. And somewhere along the way, she learned how to wield it for herself.

The first story was a little thing. A memory, almost. A girl alone in the woods. A creature that offered her power. And her answer? No. It wasn't loud. It wasn't brave. But it was firm. She was testing the waters to see how Moloch would respond to it.

Nothing. Quiet. Maybe Moloch had no real omnipresent

power he claimed to have. Maybe he was all bark, all theatre. Maybe he only worked on those already broken. Or maybe, just maybe, he didn't see her coming.

So, she wrote more. A novella about a young mother who leaves her family in the middle of the night, not out of fear or anger, but because she wants to see who she is when no one else is looking. A woman who walks not because she is chased, but because she chooses the horizon.

There was no lightning strike. No mirror cracking. Just silence. And that, in itself, was a kind of miracle. A space where her voice could live. A space he didn't seem able, or willing, to invade. So she kept going.

Then came the novel. The working title was '*Small Town*'.

That was when Moloch came to her.

Not in the mirror. Not in the shadows. In the ink. The words. The pauses between thoughts. He tried to wedge himself into her sanity. Slither through metaphors. She could feel it, the temperature in the room dropping, the strange impulse to write things she didn't believe. Lines appearing on the page that she hadn't typed. A phrase here, twisted. A motive altered. A mother becoming a monster.

She stopped typing. Waited. Whispered, "No."

He didn't like that. He looked at her like she must be kidding. She whispered, "No, this is mine." He looked at her in quiet disbelief. There was no fire and brimstone. No threat. Just silence, a heavy, bruising silence. But she could feel him. Watching. Waiting. Testing her resolve like a blade across wet rope.

They could not communicate like her husband could, but she knew, he knew, to back off.

For a while.

He came back. More forceful. Through dreams. Through her husband, pleading. Through guilt. The worst kind of manipulation, the kind that wraps itself in love.

"He begged me to leave you out of this," Moloch hissed in a dream once, his voice coming from a fox-faced woman in a red dress, one that Phillip drew earlier that day. She stood in the corner of the bedroom, barefoot, bleeding from the soles.

"He knows what you could become."

That night, the dream began like the others, familiar, warm, saturated in colours that didn't exist in the waking world. The bedroom looked the same, but wrong. The shadows had depth. The air was humid with breath that didn't belong to her. The walls pulsed, slow and steady, like lungs trying not to panic.

And then the woman appeared.

She stood in the corner, barefoot and bleeding from the soles, toes pressed into the hardwood like they were trying to root. Her red dress clung tight to her bones. Her eyes flickered between Martha's own and something just behind her, something unseen.

Her voice came slow, syrup-thick, and guttural.

"He begged me to leave you out of this."

Martha didn't speak. Couldn't. Her arms were pinned to her sides. She looked down and saw her hands weren't hers, they were soaked in ink. It dripped to the floor like oil, moving on its own. She tried to move her fingers and the black spread faster.

The woman stepped closer. Each footfall left a bloody print that hissed and disappeared. "He's scared of you," she whispered, voice breaking into three at once, her husband's, Moloch's, and a third that sounded eerily like Grace, younger. "He knows what you could become. That's why he drinks. That's why he breaks. You do that to him."

The walls behind the woman shivered. Wallpaper peeled back to reveal typewritten pages nailed into the structure like skin. Each one bore Martha's name. Not his. Hers. Then they began to burn, word by word, line by line, letters curling into ash that floated up and formed the woman's hair, long and writhing.

"He begged," the woman hissed again, falling to her knees. "He begged for me to spare you. And you repay him with silence?"

Martha found her voice then, if only in her chest. She felt the weight of the years, not as burden, but as armour. The ink on her hands stopped moving. Hardened. Became gloves of obsidian.

She looked the creature in the eye. "He made his choices."

The room groaned. A wind pressed through the cracks of the dreamscape like it was trying to escape.

The walls cracked, and from the seams poured water, slow and thick, not wet but memory, her children's laughter, the clacks of her typewriter, the taste of weak tea in the afternoon. And over it, the thing screamed.

"You will vanish. Without him, you are nothing!"

Martha tilted her head. "Then why are you here?"

The bleeding woman opened her mouth to speak, but nothing came out. Her body began to collapse inward, like something being folded wrong. One leg cracked backwards. Her spine jerked in staccato pulses. Her red dress bled black, ink pooling around her until she was just a smear across the floor.

And Martha woke.

Sheets tangled like restraints. Her mouth dry. Her chest heaving.

Then she laughed.

Not loud. Not wild. Just a small, satisfied exhale, like the last piece of a puzzle dropping into place.

Because that was the moment she knew she'd already won.

She didn't need him. Or her husband. Or anyone.

Her voice wasn't borrowed. It was forged. And it didn't tremble.

Her stories weren't about monsters. They were about girls who said no and meant it. Women who didn't wait to be saved. People who walked away. Her protagonists weren't warriors or witches or heroes, they were teachers. Janitors. Quiet ones. But they lived. They didn't sell their souls. And when the devil came calling, they didn't bargain. They weren't weak. They didn't raise swords, they closed doors. Not loudly. Not with vengeance. But with certainty.

She started building a body of work. Real stories. Stories that lived and breathed and sat with you long after the last page.

'Paddy', about a girl and her estranged mother finding each other again too late. *'One on One'*, where a female basketball coach chooses her own dignity over winning the championship. *'The Book of Rowan'*, a love story stretched across decades of misunderstanding and silence. *'Little Candles Burning'*, co-written

with Matthew McDonald, about the disposability of children in broken homes.

And always the town of Noddy's Ridge. Quiet. Slow. Alive. A place that felt like hers, even if it never really was. She could wander its streets blindfolded now, knew the cracks in the sidewalks, the rust on the mailbox flags, the weight of snow on the roofs.

She dabbled in horror sometimes. *Small Town* and *The Mouse Trap* had teeth. They bit when needed. But mostly, she wrote mainstream fiction. Deep character studies. Emotional depth. Real places. Real voices.

It wasn't long before a publisher picked up her first book. Nothing big. No billboards. No hype. But it reached the girls who needed it. Teenagers in small towns. Women with screaming children. The burnt-out. The forgotten. It wasn't about feminism. It wasn't about politics. It was about identity.

Something did gnaw at her, that it's because of her husband they picked it up, but she convinced herself she was a stand-alone author in her own right and that's what she would be. She told herself over and over again: I'm not just riding coattails. I'm stitching my own.

You don't have to be anyone's muse.

That was her message.

Not his shadow. Not his victim. Not the editor. Not the wife.

She still loved him. God help her, she did. But she wouldn't lose herself again. Not for his fame. Not for his hunger. Not for Moloch.

She wrote with the curtains open. In daylight. She didn't flinch at the mirror anymore. The kids noticed the change. Grace said she seemed taller. However, Philip kept drawing monsters. Alex sat at her feet while she worked, sometimes scribbling his own ideas.

One morning, Philip handed her a new drawing. A monster, like always. But this one was smaller. Frail. Back bent. It had wide terrified eyes, and standing in front of it was a woman. Tall. Calm. Radiant. "It's okay, Mum," he said. "This one's scared of you."

Later that night, her husband found the drawing. Stared at it for a long time. Then took it upstairs.

Three days later, he handed her something.

Just a few stapled pages. The corners dog-eared, like they'd been gripped and re-gripped too many times. No title on the front. Just a faint watermark from a spilled drink. The ink had bled slightly, like the words had sweated through the page.

He didn't say anything. Just held it out and waited until she took it.

She didn't read it straight away. Left it on the kitchen table while she rinsed dishes, wiped down the bench, rearranged the same fruit bowl twice. Then, once the kids were asleep and the silence had settled in around her like fog, she picked it up.

The story was about a creature that lived in shadows, but not the usual kind. This one changed shape, depending on who looked at it. Sometimes a man. Sometimes a child. Sometimes a voice behind a closed door. It fed on memory and spoke in riddles. It wasn't afraid of light, but it was haunted by the image of a woman. Not a warrior. Not a witch. Just a presence. A silhouette it could never touch. One it hated. Feared. Obsessively tried to unmake.

Page after page, the creature unravelled. It tried everything. Bargains, mimicry, violence. Nothing worked. The woman remained. Not fighting, not fleeing, just existing.

And that, somehow, was the worst thing of all.

She reached the end. No closure. Just the creature, curled in a corner, gnashing its teeth while the woman walked past it and shut the door.

When she looked up, he was watching her from the hallway. Not smug. Just... empty.

"You think this is me?" she asked, voice low.

He didn't look up. "Maybe. Maybe it's just a dream."

She didn't answer. Just set it on the bench and walked out of the room. The paper left a faint smear of ink on the wood.

That same week, she received her first fan letter.

A real one. Postmarked from some nowhere town in Ohio. The envelope was soft from too many hands, creased like it had been carried in a jacket pocket through rain. Blue ink smeared at the edges. No return address, just a lopsided name scrawled across the back: Jennie. No surname. No sender's address. Just the place and the paper.

Inside was a single lined sheet, torn from a school exercise book. The paper was faded yellow, the margin doodled with tiny stars and slashes. The handwriting pressed too hard in places, as though the pen might've bled mid-thought.

Dear Martha,

I hope this is okay. I don't usually write to people like this. My older sister gave me your book. Said it reminded her of me. I wasn't going to read it, but I did. Twice, actually.

The story about the girl who says no. She doesn't scream. Doesn't run. Just... says it. "No." I didn't know that could be enough. That you didn't have to fight to survive. You could just decide not to give yourself away.

I don't really know how to explain it, but I've never read something that felt like it was written by someone who'd seen inside my chest. It didn't fix anything, but it made things bearable. For a while. It made me feel like maybe I'm not ruined. Maybe I'm just waiting.
Thank you for that. Please keep writing. Please don't stop.

Sincerely,

Jennie (age 15)

P.S. I'm bad at writing but your book made me want to try.

There was a small drawing at the bottom. A crooked tree. Two girls. One standing beneath it. The other walking away, head held high.

Martha didn't move for a while. Just stared at the paper in the fading afternoon light, the sounds of the house gently ticking around her. The letter trembled slightly in her grip, like it wasn't quite ready to be real.

She thought about reading it aloud. Maybe to Grace. Maybe to herself.

Instead, she folded it, slowly, and slid it back into the envelope. She tucked it into the drawer beneath the typewriter, beside old notes, dead pens, and the scraps of herself she'd once called editing work.

Not because she didn't care.

But because she did.

Because this letter wasn't a trophy. It was proof.

That someone out there heard her voice, and answered back.

One afternoon, he caught her walking past with a galley proof of *The Mouse Trap*.

"You're publishing now?" he asked, somewhere between surprise and apology.

"Yes," she said, without looking up.

In the mirror across the room, her reflection smirked.

She passed it. Just once. Stopped. Turned. And looked.

Her face looked back.

Just hers.

She smirked. "That's what I thought."

And somewhere in the walls of the house, the darkness curled back.

Because she wasn't afraid.

Because she owned her own name and she wrote it, loud.

Chapter 11

Intervention

Martha had organised a small gathering for Friday night in a bid to inject a bit of normality into their family life. Just dinner. Just friends. For just one night when he wasn't drunk or stoned out of his mind. But long before anyone even showed up, he was eight beers in before noon, the warm buzz in his blood turning into a sharp-edged, slurring mess.

At first, he was not belligerent. He was charming, talkative, energetic, his usual brand of drunk charisma. But with each drink, his bitterness grew. By late afternoon, he was barking at Martha, barking orders to the kids, muttering under his breath when no one was listening.

When the guests arrived, the living room buzzed with small talk, the clinking of glasses, the soft hum of old friends catching up. The roasted chicken and garlic wafted through the air, warmth Martha hoped would cover the smell of failure. But then the thing she had been dreading came.

He laughed too hard at something that wasn't funny to anybody else, his voice echoing awkwardly across the room. He crashed into the coffee table, almost tipping over a tray of drinks. He leaned in too close to one of the guests, his breath cloying with beer and something sharper, more chemical… mouthwash! And when his own son later started pulling him away, he lost it.

"Don't fucking touch me," he growled, speaking low, venom-mouthed.

Those words came out across the airwaves, silencing the discussion in the room all at once. Martha's heart stopped. Everything was still, if only for a second. The air thickened and strangled what lay between them. The guests turned their heads, squirming, pretending they hadn't noticed. Grace flinched.

Alex took a step back. The agonised writer's eyes blinked slowly, as if the man realised he'd crossed the line.

Then, like every other time, he attempted to laugh it off.

"Jesus, chill out," he slurred, rubbing his face. "I was kidding. Isn't a man allowed to have a drink in his own home without all you people treating him like a damn leper?"

No one responded.

Martha disappeared down the hall. She moved quickly, not in anger, but with cold, calculated precision. A lifetime of holding things together, of excusing, explaining, justifying, and for what?

She entered his office, grabbed his wastebasket, and ripped it from its place beside his desk. The rattle of glass bottles and pill containers echoed as she stormed back into the living room. She barely felt the weight in her hands as she upended it onto the floor.

The sickening clatter of his entire secret laid bare filled the room.

A grotesque display of pills, powders, crushed-up remnants of past highs spilled out in front of their guests. Gasps rippled through the room as the true extent of his addiction was revealed. No one had realised just how bad it had become.

Martha's voice was flat, emotionless. "This is what you are now."

The struggling writer stared at the mess, stomach churning, something inside him fracturing under the strain of it all. His jaw clenched, and his hands were shaking, but not from guilt, from rage. His eyes flashed around the room, scanning their faces, reading their reactions, seeing the judgment.

"You bitch," he muttered, just above a whisper. "You really went and did this where everyone could see?" His speech wavered, caught somewhere between anger and desperation. "Real fucking nice, Martha."

She didn't blink. "You did this to yourself."

His breath came in jagged bursts, heart pounding against his ribs as the heat built. "You have no idea what I'm up against. The stress, the pressure, the work I do, "

"You mean the work that's killing you?" she interrupted, her voice chillier than he had ever heard it. "The work that's made you into this?" She indicated at the pile of drugs, then him. "You're not a writer anymore. You're not even a decent human being anymore. You're a junkie in a suit."

He flinched as if she'd shrugged him, the words hitting harder than he would allow himself to say.

"You don't get it, do you?" He jabbed a finger at her, his hands shaking, his voice quaking into the proximity of a plead. "I, I'm not your average Joe. I have responsibilities. I have, "

"You've got a choice," she interrupted him, the finality in her voice hitting him like a blow.

Rehab. Or exile.

"You walk out that door, you don't come back. Ever."

The words knocked the breath from him, left him standing there, stunned. His instinct was to fight, to deny, gaslight, manipulate, because that's what addiction had trained him to do. But then, his eyes landed on his children.

Grace stood frozen, clutching the hem of her dress, her eyes red, lips trembling. Alex refused to look up, his jaw tight, his hands shoved into his pockets like he wanted to disappear. And for the first time in years, he saw what they saw.

Not their father.

Not a writer.

Not a man worth saving.

Just a mess of a human being.

His throat closed, his stomach lurched, and something inside him collapsed in on itself. He wanted to say something, to explain, to apologise, to take it back, but what could he possibly say?

That it wasn't that bad? That they were overreacting? That he had it under control?

No one in this room would believe him anymore. Not even himself.

The fight drained out of him. His shoulders sagged, his hands dropped to his sides, his fingers twitching like they wanted to reach for something, anything, to hold onto. But there was nothing left.

"Okay," he whispered.

Martha didn't move, didn't let herself hope just yet. Her voice remained firm, steady. "Okay, what?"

His mouth was dry, the words barely making it out.

"Okay," he said again. "I'll go."

And just like that, it was over.

But something lingered in the shady back alley of his mind.

Moloch, distant yet watching.

The author believed he would soon be free from Moloch's control.

The withdrawals were worse than anything he had imagined. He had expected the usual horrors, the tremors, the nausea, the paranoia, but this? This was something else. Something unnatural.

The doctors at the rehab centre chalked it up to delirium tremens, a common side effect of detoxing from years of alcohol and cocaine abuse. They thought his brain was simply recalibrating, purging the toxins, struggling to function without the poisons it had relied on for so long.

But they were wrong.

This wasn't withdrawal.

This was Moloch clawing at the inside of his skull, furious at being cast out.

It had been two weeks since his last fix, and the staff had begun reducing his sedatives in an attempt to transition him into therapy. The shakes were still there, but the worst of the physical detox had passed. That was when the visions started.

At first, it was just a sensation, a presence in the room, something shifting in the shadows of the rehab centre's fluorescent lights. Then, in the quiet hours of the night, he saw him.

A man, or something wearing a man's skin, stretched unnaturally across the ceiling, its long, skeletal limbs bracing against the corners of the room like a grotesque spider. Its face was twisted, wrong, its mouth too wide, its teeth too many, its eyes black as oil.

It never moved when he looked at it directly.

But the moment he blinked, it inched closer.

The nurses found him the next morning huddled under his

bed, his fingernails torn and bloody from clawing at the floor, whispering over and over, "He's in the ceiling. He's in the fucking ceiling. He's watching. Don't blink. Don't let him get closer."

They had to restrain him just to get him back into bed.

That night, the same thing happened. The nurses strapped him down to keep him from injuring himself, but when they checked on him at 3 AM, they found him still screaming, eyes bloodshot, convulsing against the leather restraints.

Martha received a phone call the next morning.

"We've had patients go through detox psychosis before," the doctor said hesitantly. "But this… this is different. He's not just hallucinating, something is gripping onto him, like it's pulling him apart at the seams. If this continues, we'll have no choice but to recommend sectioning him under the Mental Health Act. Right now, he's not just a danger to himself, he's a danger to everyone around him."

After his episode with the ceiling man, they increased his medication to keep him sedated. It worked, for a time. But eventually, as the drugs wore off, he began telling stories.

At first, the nurses thought it was a good sign. He was a writer, after all. If he was talking, maybe it meant he was coming back to himself.

They were wrong.

The stories he told weren't normal.

They weren't fiction.

They were things that had never been spoken aloud before, things that should have never been known.

He spoke of creatures that crawled beneath the floors, whispering the names of the dead. He described a man with a hole in his chest, where something black and writhing had burrowed inside. He told them about a woman who sewed her own eyes shut so that she wouldn't see what waited for her at the edge of the world.

And he spoke of Moloch.

"He's still with me," he told the other patients. "Even now. Even here. He's watching me through the mirrors. He's whispering in my ear while I sleep. You think you're safe here?

You think the walls keep him out?"

By the end of the first week, three patients relapsed out of sheer terror. One woman tried to dig out her own ears, screaming that she could hear what was coming through the walls. Another man suffered a full psychotic break, convinced something had entered his bloodstream, burrowing its way into his organs.

The hospital staff could no longer ignore it.

The stories were spreading like a sickness.

"He's scaring the other patients," one of the orderlies told Martha in hushed, frantic tones. "We can't control him. He doesn't just talk about these things, he makes people believe them. He looks at you, and it's like you can see it too."

The next day, they transferred him to an isolated room and barred him from group therapy.

The isolation room was sterile. White walls. No windows. The faint scent of antiseptic clung to the air, stinging his nostrils. The bed beneath him was hard, barely a mattress at all, designed for safety, not comfort. The door had no handle on the inside. He was locked in.

At first, the silence was unbearable. No whispers, no scratching at the edges of his mind. Moloch was absent. That should have been a relief, but it only made the paranoia worse. The silence was a trick. A game.

Then the room changed.

Not in any obvious way at first. The walls breathed, expanding and contracting like lungs. The ceiling lights flickered, harsh, clinical. They weren't alone. They were watching.

He sat up and realized he wasn't in the rehab centre anymore.

A nurse stood by the door, her figure towering, arms crossed. A starched white uniform. A cap that sat perfectly atop her neatly styled hair. A name tag pinned to her chest.

His breath caught. No. That wasn't right.

A mirror hung in the room now, where there had been none before. His own reflection leered back at him, but it wasn't him. Randle McMurphy stared out at him. The smirk. The defiance. The exhaustion hidden behind it all. The man who refused to be broken.

"Time for your meds, Mr. McMurphy," Nurse Ratched said, her voice sweet like arsenic.

His heartbeat thudded against his ribs.

Not real. This isn't real.

"You're not gonna get the best of me," he sneered, throwing her a cocky grin, McMurphy's grin, not his own.

She smiled, patient. Controlled. A smile that said, Oh, but I already have.

"You're confused, dear. You don't belong in the world anymore, don't you see that? You belong here. Where we can keep you safe."

She approached, slow and deliberate, a paper cup in hand, filled with little white pills.

"Open up," she said.

His fists clenched. He wasn't going to take the goddamn pills. He wasn't going to be sedated, wasn't going to be turned into some drooling vegetable like the others.

He turned his head and the room expanded. Rows of beds, filled with men whose spirits had been sucked dry. Eyes vacant. Mouths slack. Cheeks sunken from years of compliance.

Chief Bromden sat in the corner, staring straight ahead, watching but never speaking.

No. No, no, no.

He grabbed at his hair, at his own skin, digging his nails into his arm, trying to claw himself back into reality.

"You're not real," he whispered.

Nurse Ratched clicked her tongue.

"Of course I'm real, dear. Now, are you going to be good and take your medicine? Or do we have to do this the hard way?"

The hard way. Electroshock.

The room tilted, shifted, and he was strapped to a table. Leather restraints pinned him down. The bright lights above buzzed like angry wasps. The smell of something burning.

A doctor leaned over him, a metal contraption in his hands.

"This won't hurt a bit."

The machine roared to life.

His body arched, pain ripping through his skull, through his bones, then he was back.

Back in the isolation room, sweating through his clothes, his body convulsing as if the electricity had followed him out of the hallucination. His pulse raced, his chest heaved, his fingers curled into the sheets like he was still trying to fight them off.

The door opened. A real nurse, not Ratched, just a woman in navy scrubs, stepped inside.

She didn't speak at first, just studied him warily, like a handler stepping into a cage with a wild animal.

"Are you alright?" she asked, cautious.

The question made him laugh. A sharp, bitter sound.

"Yeah," he said. "I'm just dandy."

She frowned. "Your heart rate's through the roof. Do you want something to help you sleep?"

His throat was dry as dust. "What I want is to get the fuck out of here."

The nurse sighed. "We'll see how you do in the next few days."

She left him alone.

For the first time, he wondered if he'd ever really get out at all.

The shift was so sudden, so complete, that even the doctors were stunned.

For weeks, the author had been trapped in his isolated room, confined like a violent inmate. The nurses entered only when necessary, always in pairs, always cautious, because he was unpredictable, thrashing, whispering, clawing at unseen horrors. But then, as if a switch had been flipped, he went quiet.

The manic fits ceased. The screaming at night stopped. The hallucinations, at least, the ones they could observe, vanished.

And the most shocking change of all?

He smiled.

Not the wild, desperate grin of a man losing his grip, but a tired, almost peaceful expression, like a drowning man finally breaking the surface.

Then, he slept.

For the first time in years, true, unbroken sleep claimed him. At first, the doctors and nurses worried, was he slipping into a coma? Had the final crash of withdrawal shut down his system entirely? But his vitals were stable, his breathing deep and steady. His body had simply reached its limit. The storm had passed, leaving him shipwrecked, and now he had to recover.

For an entire week, he barely stirred.

No outbursts. No restless thrashing. No nightmares that sent him screaming into the halls. Just sleep, deep, heavy, dreamless.

His body was rebuilding itself, piece by piece, trying to recover from the last four weeks of agony, but more than that, from the decades of abuse that had worn him down to nothing. Decades of poisoning his own mind. Decades of being consumed by something beyond himself.

The nurses tiptoed around his room, reluctant to disturb whatever fragile peace he had finally found. When Martha visited, she sat at his bedside, watching the slow rise and fall of his chest, trying to believe, really believe, that this meant something. That this was the beginning of something better.

On the eighth day, he woke.

The doctors saw progress. The nurses felt safe around him again. Martha, when she visited, no longer looked at him with fear and exhaustion, but with cautious hope.

And so, they moved him back to the general ward.

"I think I'm getting better," he told Dr Harris during one of their sessions. "I feel… clearer. Lighter. Like something's finally let me go."

Dr Harris observed him carefully, tapping his pen against the edge of his notepad. "No more hallucinations?"

"No more."

"And Moloch?"

For the first time in years, the author said it with conviction:

"He's gone."

The relief in the room was palpable.

After some more consultations they moved him back to the general ward.

The transition was slow, monitored carefully, controlled, but it felt like the first real step toward recovery. Gone were the leather restraints, the isolation, the whispered conversations behind glass. Now, he sat among the other patients, eating meals in the common room, attending group therapy, engaging in structured activities.

Dr Harris suggested writing therapy, believing that reconnecting with his craft without Moloch's influence could be the final step in his recovery.

For days, the suggestion haunted him.

Dr Harris had mentioned it casually, as if it were just another step in recovery, but the idea of writing without Moloch sent a cold pulse of dread through the author's chest.

"It was always your gift," Harris had said. "It doesn't have to be a curse."

But what if it was never his gift at all?

The thought clung to him like a parasite, whispering at the edges of his mind. What if Moloch had always been the real writer? What if, without him, the words would never come again?

He sat alone in his room, staring at the blank notebook Dr Harris had left him, his fingers tracing the spine like it was a loaded gun.

What if he put pen to paper and nothing happened?

What if the page stayed empty, mocking him?

Or worse, what if he wrote something and it was garbage? What if the stories, the ones that had once flowed like blood from a wound, were now just flat, dead things?

He could hear Moloch's voice, distant but taunting:

"You were never great. I was great. You were just the hand that held the pen."

A sharp knock on the door startled him.

Martha stepped inside, hesitant but determined. She glanced at the untouched notebook on his lap, then at the distant look in his eyes. She knew that look, the fear of irrelevance, the fear of failure, the fear of facing himself without the crutch of darkness.

She sat down across from him, waiting until he met her gaze.

"I can't do it, I can't even write my own name, I feel like such a fraud" he admitted, his voice barely above a whisper.

Martha frowned. "Why?"

He exhaled shakily. "What if I was never a real writer? What if it was always him? What if I try and, " His breath hitched. ", there's nothing left?"

She studied him for a long moment before reaching forward, placing her hand over his.

"Then we find out together."

His throat tightened.

"You don't have to do this alone," she said softly. "I'll help you try. We'll start small. Just a sentence. Just one. And if it's awful, who cares? You can write another one. And another."

He looked down at the notebook again, his fingers still frozen.

"But if you don't try," Martha continued, "then Moloch wins. And I don't think you want that."

He swallowed hard, his grip on the pen tightening.

Maybe she was right.

Maybe he had to fight for it.

Maybe, just maybe, he could be something without Moloch after all.

With Martha watching, waiting, believing in him, he put the pen to paper.

And he wrote.

For the first time in years, he wrote without feeling something looming over his shoulder. The words came slow, hesitant, uncertain. But they came. He let himself believe, just for a moment, that the nightmare was over.

The kitchen held its breath in half-light. Fluorescent hum. Cold tile beneath her bare feet. Shadows climbed the ceiling in long, reaching fingers. Martha didn't move. Behind her, the reflection in the window no longer mirrored her shape. It lagged, like memory. Or possession.

A voice, unseen, sifted through the silence.

'You shouldn't be awake.'

She didn't turn. 'You shouldn't be here.'

Closer now. Low and scorched.

'You opened the door. You read the words. You let me in.'

'I didn't let you in,' she said. 'You were already inside him. I just saw the mess you made.'

He took shape behind her, half-coal, half-crown, skin aglow with ember-light under cracked stone. Moloch. But not whole. There was something missing, something vital. The furnace god gone brittle with grief.

'He was mine,' he said. 'A perfect vessel. Desperate. Brilliant. Hollow.'

Then, softer: 'But you, you're something else.'

She turned. Steady. Jaw set.

'You can't bend me. That's why you hate me. Admit it.'

A twitch of his cracked lips.

'Hate? No. Fear.'

He stepped forward, fire whispering beneath his ribs.

'And not of you, little spine of iron and grief. No. It's what walks behind you. The one who filled your lungs with defiance. Who whispered stand when you should have wept.'

Her eyes narrowed. 'You're bluffing. You're scared of me because I didn't break.'

He leaned in. Voice dropped to a hiss.

'You're the side effect. The consequence. But not the cause.'

He dragged one clawed finger through the air. Sparks bled from it, burnt constellations in reverse.

'Do you know why I crave destruction?' he asked. 'Why I hollow out men and let them echo?'

Martha didn't blink. 'Because you're a sadistic cunt?'

His eyes glowed.

'Because they took her from me. My wife. My flame. Ishat. Gutted by Anat the war goddess. Do you understand what that did to a god of fire?'

The temperature shifted. A warmth stirred behind Martha. Something unseen. Something watching.

His voice cracked, low with something that might once have been sorrow.

'They turned me to ash. And now I burn you. All of you. Your children. Your art. Your hope. Every love is a pyre. Every promise, kindling.'

He stared at her, no longer furious, only hollow.

'But you...'

His gaze flicked to the space behind her, uncertain.

'You walk with something older than me. Something the gods fear.'

Martha tilted her head, almost smiling.

'I thought it was just my effervescent personality?'

Moloch stepped back.

'You never stood alone. You lit a candle, and something walked through the smoke. Not a god. Not a shadow. Something that remembers when I was new.'

She looked at her hands. For a moment, her skin shimmered, not flame, but stars.

'Then maybe you should leave,' she said softly.

His grin twisted, ash falling from the corners.

'Oh, I will. But when it wakes up... don't thank me for the warning. Thank me for being the lesser thing in the dark.'

And he was gone. A hiss of air. Ash scattered in the light.

The kitchen steadied.

Martha stood alone.

Or thought she did.

From the hallway behind her, something exhaled. Not breath. Not quite presence. Just the sound of something waiting.

Had Moloch truly gone?

She hoped so.

But she hadn't seen it. Not yet.

Our author didn't notice how, when he picked up the pen, his reflection in the window lagged just a second behind.

He didn't hear the almost imperceptible chuckle curling through the quiet, like a whisper of smoke.

Didn't realise that hope was just another illusion Moloch had crafted for him.

The game wasn't over.

It had only just begun.

Without Moloch whispering in his ear, the silence felt like mourning. Simple and quiet. Each word was as painful as the rehab itself. He tried writing without the darkness, without the rush of something unnatural guiding his hands. But the words felt dead on the page. Flat. Hollow. Like he had no voice of his own.

Moloch had always been a parasite, a leech on his creative subconscious. But now, after the intervention, after the sobering crash of reality, it had evolved.

The author thought he'd cut the entity out like a tumour. But tumours leave shadows behind.

The meeting took place in Dr. Harris's office, the blinds half-drawn, the faint hum of conversation and rolling gurneys just beyond the door. The air smelled of old coffee and disinfectant.

Martha sat across from Dr. Harris, her hands clasped tightly together in her lap. The author sat beside her, stiff, unreadable, his eyes fixed on the desk like it held some terrible secret.

Dr. Harris flipped through the manila file. "Medically speaking, he's stable," he said finally. "No more acute withdrawal symptoms. No more psychotic episodes, at least, none we've observed." He glanced up, expression cautious. "That said, I won't lie to you. I'm hesitant."

Martha inhaled sharply. "Hesitant?"

"The risk of relapse is high. And I don't mean just substance abuse." He looked at the author now. "You're an addict, yes. But more than that, you're dependent on something else, something we can't diagnose, something we can't treat with medication."

The author shifted in his chair. His hands twitched in his lap, fingers flexing against an invisible pen. "You think I'm still seeing things."

Dr. Harris leaned forward. "Are you?"

A pause.

"No," he said. A lie.

Dr. Harris studied him for a long moment, then sighed. "Look. You've made progress, more than I expected, but healing doesn't end when you walk out of here. The real challenge starts the moment you step back into your old life."

Martha nodded, but her grip on her own fingers tightened. "What do you suggest?"

"A structured environment. Keep him on routine. No isolation.

No long hours locked in his office, alone with his thoughts." He paused. "And if the hallucinations return, if Moloch comes back, you bring him straight back here."

The words sat heavy in the room.

The author let out a slow breath. He had expected relief at the idea of leaving, but instead, there was only dread, thick and crawling under his skin.

Leaving the hospital meant going home.

Going home meant proving himself.

And proving himself meant facing the fact that he might still be broken.

Martha nodded. "We'll do whatever it takes."

Dr. Harris hesitated before closing the file. "Then, as far as the hospital is concerned, you're free to go."

On his way out, duffle bag slung over his shoulder, the author found himself stalling outside the common room.

Inside, the other patients were watching TV, playing cards, staring at the walls like ghosts who hadn't yet decided if they were going to move on.

He wasn't sure why he was looking for him.

And then, there he was.

Peter.

The old man had been in the hospital long before the author arrived and would likely be there long after. He was frail but sharp, with a pale, weathered face and hollow, knowing eyes. He had been the only one to talk to the author like he was still human during the worst of his psychosis. The only one who hadn't been afraid.

The author approached slowly, his presence casting a shadow over Peter's chessboard. The old man glanced up, a tired smile tugging at his lips.

"So," Peter said. "They finally kicking you out?"

The author smirked. "Guess so."

Peter moved a knight across the board. "You ready for it?"

"Hell if I know."

Peter studied him for a moment, then chuckled. "Well, you weren't ready for this place either, and you survived that."

The author huffed a laugh but felt no humour in it.

Peter's gaze darkened. "The voices gone?"

"Yeah." Another lie.

Peter didn't call him on it. He just nodded, looking back at the board. "Well. If you ever come back, I'll still be here."

The author swallowed. "Hope I don't."

Peter smiled at that, but it was sad. "Me too, kid. Me too."

The author reached out, squeezing Peter's shoulder. Peter didn't flinch. That meant something.

Then, with a final nod, the author turned and walked away.

The hallway stretched before him, impossibly long. Each step felt heavier than the last.

The exit doors loomed ahead.

A nurse stood by them, clipboard in hand. She smiled politely as he approached. "Good luck out there," she said.

He nodded, barely glancing at her, reaching for the door,

And then, just for a second, her face shifted.

The smile widened too much. The edges of her eyes tightened into something cruel. Her hair darkened, her pristine uniform taking on a harsher, starched crispness.

Nurse Ratched.

Then, gone.

He blinked rapidly, his pulse hammering.

The nurse, the real nurse, Nurse Jean was looking at him, frowning slightly. "Sir? Are you alright?"

He forced a breath. Forced a nod. Swallowed the nausea clawing up his throat.

"Yeah," he rasped. "Fine."

He pushed through the doors into the blinding light of the outside world.

And for the first time since he could remember, he had no idea if what he had just seen was real or not.

The homecoming wasn't a celebration. It wasn't a moment of healing. It was a test.

The kids were there, but they weren't really there. He could feel it in the small ways, how Alex never met his eyes for too long, how Grace's smile was forced, tight at the edges, like she was performing normalcy. Like they all were.

At dinner, they spoke to Martha, not him. When they left the room, they left together, like an unspoken rule had formed between them.

Even the air in the house had changed.

It wasn't just his paranoia, they were watching him.

Waiting.

For what? For him to fall apart again?

For the first few days, he convinced himself it was just adjustment. That time would fix it. That soon, Grace would curl up beside him with a book like she used to. That Alex would stop flinching when he raised his voice, hell, when he so much as spoke.

But time passed, and nothing changed. The only one that gave him any love was Philip, and that's only because he was too young to know any better.

Martha told him to be patient. But patience didn't make it easier. Patience didn't stop the resentment from curdling inside him.

They don't trust me.

And maybe they never would.

And maybe... maybe they were right not to.

He hated them for it.

But he loved them, too.

And that was the cruellest part.

The absence of Moloch was unsettling, like a missing limb still itching in the dark. Writing became a struggle, every word forced, wooden, lacking the fire that had once made his prose pulse with life. He sat in front of his typewriter, fingers hovering uselessly, and realised with growing horror that without Moloch, he was nothing.

But Moloch had not left.

It had simply changed tactics.

It no longer whispered in the dead of night, no longer filled his mind with feverish visions that sent him scrambling for a pen. Instead, it crept into his dreams. At first, the nightmares were indistinct, a weight pressing on his chest, suffocating him in the dark. Then they became clearer.

Moloch manifested as a clown covered with spiders in his dreams, torturing him, proving that it could take any form. A shadow stood at the foot of his bed, flickering like a candle flame, watching. Silent.

When he woke, the presence lingered, an oily residue in the back of his mind.

Then the strange occurrences began.

Lights flickering in his study whenever he tried to write. Pages of half-finished manuscripts curling at the edges as though burned, though he never touched a match. His typewriter producing words he did not remember writing, sentences that did not sound like his own.

Then, one morning, he found an entire chapter completed in his latest manuscript. The prose was perfect, electric, exactly what he had been struggling to achieve. He read it twice before realising:

He hadn't written a single word of it.

The voices returned. Not in the chaotic, fevered whispers of before, but in a subtler, more insidious form. "You don't need the drugs anymore. You just need me." "Let me guide your hands." "Your words were never yours to begin with." It wasn't just in his mind. The world around him started to shift. He knew he could not admit to anyone what was happening, they'd surely lock me up and throw away the key if they knew.

Martha found him staring at his reflection in the bathroom mirror for hours at a time, unblinking, his lips moving as if in conversation. But when she asked him what he was saying, he had no memory of speaking at all. His children, who once avoided him because of his drinking, now avoided him for another reason. They whispered to each other when they thought he wasn't listening. Their father was different. Not angry, not drunk. Just… wrong. Even the air in the house felt different. Stagnant. Heavy.

Moloch had evolved, embedding itself deeper, subtler. Not a voice in his ear, but a presence in his very skin, in his bones, in the spaces between his thoughts. He no longer craved drugs, but he craved something else, a hunger that gnawed at him, a need to put words to the page, any words, just to keep the silence at bay. And Moloch was there. Always waiting. Always watching. And now, it had all the time in the world.

Chapter 12

Might as Well Be Dead

The author, MY author, has become all too dull, a wasted husk of the man he once was. There was no fire left, no desperate hunger to create, no nights spent on the edge of madness, pushing the boundaries of reality. Sobriety had hollowed him out, leaving him predictable, routine-bound, and utterly useless.

And what about you? Sitting there, eyes scanning the page. Do you feel safe? Tucked behind your book, in your dimly lit room, under the covers, perhaps? Do you think yourself superior? Detached? Observing from a distance, thinking yourself different from him? I can assure you, you're not. There's a reason you're still here, isn't there? A reason you keep turning the page, feeding off the sickness, drinking down the madness like it won't leave a stain. Your inability to look away from a deranged body at the scene of an accident.

Maybe you tell yourself it's just a story. Just fiction. Nothing seeps through the cracks; nothing lingers in the spaces between the words. So go on. Keep reading. Keep telling yourself you're only watching. You don't hear me yet, do you? But you will. I'll wait. I have all the time in the world.

The partnership had once been exhilarating. Moloch had whispered stories into his ear, filling his veins with inspiration as he drank himself into oblivion, as he tore through lines of powder that cracked open his mind like a gaping wound. The man had once been willing to pay any price for brilliance. But now? Now, he goes for walks. Walks! Every day, the same four miles. The same silence where Moloch's voice once thrived. He was getting old, weak, dull, a dry chat even. Moloch had grown weary. Not with anger, not with hate, just the slow, inevitable disinterest of a being beyond time. A god does not throw tantrums. A god does not sulk. A god simply ceases to care. And when gods decide to leave, they do not go quietly. And Moloch didn't disappoint. The idea came easily, as all good ones do. It was just a matter of timing, and today the timing was perfect.

The author, as always, was out for his afternoon walk, clearing his head before an evening with his family. He's taking his family to the movies later, but always the walk. Every day. The routine. That fucking walk. And then, there was the driver. An idiot that only sees the world from his perspective, another junkie. Moloch loves junkies, they're so malleable, so easily twisted. Wasted space meant to be used and abused for his, for our pleasure. Barry was driving his 1985 Dodge Caravan, distracted, one hand on the wheel, the other swiping at the Rottweiler in the back, who whined and scrabbled at the cooler box filled with all the goods. The dog, Bullet, was his name; restless, agitated, was just looking for food. Moloch gave it something else. A nudge. A whisper. A pulse of something deep and primal. The dog froze, ears flattening, muscles coiling tight. A low, trembling growl vibrated in its throat, not at Barry, but at something else. Something it could see or sense but could not understand. Its pupils shrank to pinpricks, hackles rising, body torn between fight and flight. Then, Moloch twisted the fear into hunger. And Bullet lunged.

Smith reacted instantly, leaning back, twisting in his seat to calm the dog down, his attention torn away from the road for just a second. A second is all it took. The van veered sharply, tyres skidding on the pavement. The Dodge Caravan crested the hill too fast. The driver wasn't looking. The road stretched ahead, a lazy ribbon of blacktop baking under the summer sun. He walked it every day, habit more than anything, a ritual to break up the hours between writing and the vague disquiet that came with being alone too long in his own mind. He had done this for years. Fucken' years. It had been a good week, thought the author to himself. The house was full of voices, laughter, the warmth of his children, their spouses, and his grandchild, a three-month-old bundle of joy, wide-eyed wonder. The kind of week that made him forget, ever so briefly, the things he had given up in exchange for the words. Oh, the words. The stories. He had just enough time to stretch his legs before the evening plans, the air thick with the scent of pine needles and the lake in the distance, a promise of a cooler night's walk if he stayed out long enough.

Not long after passing the crest he never saw the van coming. In a single moment, he was walking, mindful of the shifting gravel beneath his feet. In the next, a blur of light-blue metal, a flash of movement, a sudden wrongness, and the thought entered his mind: My God, I'm going to die.

The van slammed into him at 45 miles an hour, folding his body around the hood like a ragdoll, lifting him from the ground in a cartoonish arc. His right leg snapped instantly, the femur shattering like brittle glass. His hip fractured under the force, and his pelvis crushed in ways that would never truly heal. Ribs cracked, bone splintering inward, one jagged edge piercing a lung. When awareness returned, he was on the ground, 14 feet in the air, then another 14 in the ditch, looking at the rear of the van as if someone had placed him there for a better view. Dust curled lazily around its taillights. His body felt unfamiliar, disconnected, as though it belonged to someone else. There was blood. So much of it.

Barry was sitting beside him now. Perched on a nearby rock, cane balanced across his lap like he was waiting for a train that would never come, his expression... motionless, almost bemused at the absurdity of the situation. "Ain't we both just had the shittiest luck?" his face frozen solid. He'd thought he'd hit a deer until he spotted the spectacles lying in the front seat of his van, lenses unbroken, frames twisted. The pain hit the author in waves, jagged and sickly. His leg was wrong, grotesquely twisted as if some careless god had wrenched it sideways. Please let it just be dislocated. He forced the words out through cracked lips. "Nah," Smith said, voice too cheery, as if they were discussing a baseball game. "Broken in five, maybe six places."

The world swam. A siren howled in the distance, growing louder. The crunch of tyres on gravel. A man in an EMT uniform kneeling beside him now, words coming slow, deliberate as if they could be chewed and swallowed like dry bread. "You're gonna be okay. What's your name?" He gave it. He remembered his wife. His children. The house was so full of life just hours ago. He asked for a cigarette. The EMT laughed. "Not hardly."

The pain was total. A symphony of shattered nerves and torn flesh, every synapse in his body screaming in unison, a choir of agony that drowned out thought and all reason. He was nothing but pain, a being reduced to suffering, no past, no future, just the raw, burning now. And then, a shift. Something peeled away from him.

For a fleeting moment, the author thought he was watching his own soul detach, some final unspooling of life before the darkness swallowed him whole. It felt like the air itself was being sucked from his lungs, as though the very essence of him was being wrenched free, leaving behind only the ruin of a man who used to be something. But it wasn't his soul. No, this was something else.

Moloch stood there, whole and unburdened, no longer tethered to the flesh and blood he had coiled himself around for so many years. He loomed above the broken author, an outline too sharp, too defined, like the shadow of a man cast in reverse, light bleeding out instead of in. His form flickered at the edges, an afterimage on the retina that pulsed in and out of reality, his presence both there and not. The author lay in the trolly on pavement, chest rising in ragged, shallow bursts, watching. Moloch did not move at first. He just looked at him. And that was the worst part. The look.

It wasn't anger. Not entirely. Nor was it disappointment. Not fully. It wasn't even pity, though it carried a cruel whisper of it, like an insect crawling at the edge of something rotting. It was the cold detachment of a god surveying a failed creation. His lips curled slightly, just a fraction. Not quite a smirk, not quite a sneer. His head tilted as if this moment fascinated him as if he was waiting for something that hadn't come. For the author to do something, anything. But he didn't. He just lay there. Broken. Like the weak man he'd become. That's all you were? The look seemed to say. That's all you amounted to?

Moloch built him up from nothing, filled his veins with fire, made his name ring in the mouths of the living for decades. He had been a conduit, a masterpiece of obsession and decay, his stories laced with something older than language, something that made people shudder without knowing why. But look at him now. All that time, all that potential, wasted. Pathetic. Moloch's fingers twitched. A phantom urge, maybe. To reach down? To rip open his chest and dig for something still worth keeping? To see if there was a shred of him left, buried beneath the frailty, beneath the brittle bones and sagging flesh? A thought. Nothing more. Because there was nothing worth keeping.

Moloch inhaled a long, slow breath as if tasting the air one last time. He had fed on his fears, his doubts, his addictions, his surrender, his compliance for so long even he's disappointed. And now, there was nothing left to take. Nothing left to feed off. Nothing left to care about. The author opened his mouth to speak, but no sound came. His throat was raw, his body too weak to form words. Maybe he really had nothing to say anyway. Moloch gave a quiet nod. Not of respect. Not of farewell. It was a dismissal. Then he turned, not in a rush, not in triumph. Just a smooth, effortless motion. He walked, his form stretching and flickering in the dim light, his silhouette growing thinner, taller until he was nothing but a smudge against the horizon. And then, over the crest of the hill, and gone. Untethered. Done.

And for the first time in decades, the writer was alone. Truly alone. Pain spiked again as hands moved over his ruined leg. Voices blurred. A stretcher. A jolt of agony so sharp he screamed, a raw animal sound. The world narrowed, dimmed, vanished. When he surfaced, he was inside an ambulance, wheels hammering over the patched tarmac at breakneck speed. "Do you swear to God?" he rasped. "That I'll be okay?" The EMT hesitated just long enough for doubt to seep through. There was a helicopter. The deafening whap-whap-whap of rotors cutting through the thick, humid air. They lifted him, careful but not careful enough, and he cried out as fresh agony lanced through his shattered frame.

"Ever been in a chopper before?" a voice bellowed over the noise. He tried to answer but couldn't; his lungs weren't working right. I feel like I'm drowning. "Shit, his lungs collapsed," someone said. How did that get missed? then a rattle of paper and the opening of sterilised equipment. The feeling of something pressing, cutting, sliding between ribs. A whistle of air, a sudden, shocking relief. His body was failing him, one by one his systems start shutting down, but he wasn't ready to go. Not yet. Not like this. Frantically, he was looking for him. Pushing through the haze of pain, the dead weight of his shattered body, he searched the shadows for some trace, some lingering ember of what had been there. His lips moved, dry and cracked, forming the name. "Moloch."

The paramedic beside him frowned. "What was that? Stay with me, buddy." "Moloch," he tried but only rasped again, and their faces remained blank, unreadable. As if they hadn't heard. As if the name itself had dissolved before reaching their ears. "He's confused," one of them muttered. "Shock setting in." He tried again, but this time, he wasn't sure what came out. His tongue twisted, syllables bending into something broken, something unintelligible. His mind screamed the name, but all that escaped his lips was nonsense, gibberish, incoherent, meaningless.

At the hospital, the lights blurred past overhead, causing him to want to throw up. Voices, distant, orders barked, echoing, the echoes bouncing throughout his throbbing head was all he had to tell him he was still alive. A memory surfaced, he had been planning to pick berries earlier, before the film, during the walk down by the lake. But now he was here, suspended between life and oblivion. He fought to hold on; oh god, he fought. Time twisted with each blink. Surgery. More surgery. Waking to pain so complete it was almost a presence, a replacement for Moloch. His wife, her hands cool against his fevered skin. The fight to move. To stand. To reclaim some sliver of his former self.

The first time it happened, he was staring at the blank page in front of him, the weight of the pen unfamiliar in his trembling fingers. The words came sluggishly, reluctant, as if they knew they no longer belonged to him. He forced them onto the page, scrawling in uneven, fevered strokes, trying to exorcise something unseen. He had to learn to write again. Then the ink began to move.

At first, it was subtle. A slow crawl, the letters bleeding into one another, shifting unnaturally, rearranging themselves into words he hadn't written. And then, one peeled away from the page. A tiny black speck, a dot of ink that detached itself, legs unfurling from the smudge as it skittered across the paper. A spider! Then another. Then another. The words themselves unravelled into writhing, living things, the paper birthing them in obscene numbers, their ink-drenched legs scurrying toward him, up his fingers, beneath his nails, burrowing into his flesh.

He screamed. They poured up his arms, into his eyes, his mouth, his nose. Millions of them, biting, biting, biting. He could feel them beneath his skin, scratching, crawling, gnawing at his sanity. Each bite rotted away a piece of him, black necrosis spreading beneath his flesh. He clawed at his skin, his face, trying to tear them out, tear himself apart, purge them from his body. Moloch knew. Moloch knew what he feared most. He couldn't help but torment him.

The door burst open. A nurse grabbed him, hands pinning his arms down as he thrashed violently, another went for his feet, his movements were too strong until an imposing 6'5" orderly that had the build of a line-backer, broad-shouldered, solid as a rock, and moving with the quiet confidence of someone who knew his strength but didn't need to prove it. His deep brown skin contrasted with the crisp white of his uniform, and despite his size, there was a steadiness in his movements, a practiced ease that put patients at ease. Not this time. He meant business.

His screams raw, animalistic. "Get them off me! Get them off me!" "There's nothing there!" a deep southern voice shouted, but he didn't believe it. He felt them, deep inside, nesting in the hollowed-out spaces where Moloch had once been. Night after night the nightmares didn't stop. Night after night, the spiders returned. They lived inside him, hatched from his words, feasted on his sanity. The hospital bed became a nest, the sheets a web.

He stopped sleeping, afraid to close his eyes, afraid of what would come next.

After a few days of this chaotic scene replaying each time he tried to sleep they called in a specialist. A soft-spoken man with round glasses and a clipboard, the kind of face built for delivering bad news in a voice that made it sound tolerable. "We need to talk about your pain management." He already knew what that meant. No painkillers, no sedatives, no drugs. The doctors and Martha both thought he'd relapse if he had any, thought he'd crawl back to the bottle, the pills, or worse... the powder. "I can't sleep," the author rasped. "Every time I close my eyes, they come back." The doctor exchanged a glance with Martha, who stood by the door, arms crossed. She looked concerned, but not in the way he needed her to be. Not in the way that meant she believed him. "We'll try something mild," the doctor said. "A low-dose sedative, just to help you rest."

The first round of pills arrived that night, small white ones that clattered into his palm. He swallowed them greedily, desperate for escape, for oblivion. A week passed by. Eventually the spiders stopped reaching for him. For the first time since the accident, he finally felt at peace. He slept unrepentantly, the weight of his own thoughts no longer pressing against his skull. Then, one evening, he overheard them talking.

Martha and the doctor, outside his room, voices hushed but not quite hushed enough. "They're just placebos," the doctor said. "Nothing more than Tic Tacs." Silence. Then Martha's voice, hesitant. "And you think it's working?" "He believes it is." His stomach turned. His pulse pounded in his skull. The relief had been a lie. He wasn't free of Moloch's talons. They had only convinced him he was. Voices, distant, echoing. He wasn't convinced he was hearing them right, he thought maybe it was the drugs playing tricks on his mind.

Time continued to twist. Surgery. More surgery. Waking to pain was his life now. He could feel Martha's hands cool against his fevered skin each time he came out of surgery. It gave him the fight to move. To stand. To reclaim some sliver of his former self. Days later as he's coming off yet another surgery he sees his new next door neighbour in the ward as he's walking down the corridor with the physiotherapist. Libbie. A sexy woman with him in rehab? The drugs must be working, shuffling forward one stubborn step at a time. "Your slip's showing," he joked, voice strained. "Your ass is showing." She grinned, wheezing. He laughed for the first time since the accident.

It was moments like this that helped him fight on. A sense of normalcy. No one cared who he was in here, they just cared about who he will be out there.

Much to his ego's disappointment the world outside moved on, uncaring, but inside the hospital walls, he fought for inches, feet, and moments. By July, he was wheeled outside to watch fireworks burst against the summer sky, Martha's hand in his, grounding him. He had survived. The days stretched. Physical therapy was brutal, each session a slow war between what his body could handle and what the therapists insisted it could take. They pushed him hard, too hard sometimes, offering tight-lipped encouragement while watching him wince, their smiles never quite reaching their eyes. The fixator was now gone, but the pain oh the pain lingered, deep within his bones, impacting every fibre, driven into every breath. Nights were the worst. He'd wake drenched in sweat, tangled in the sheets, his pulse hammering, the phantom echo of the impact still rattling inside his skull. He dreaded sleep almost as much as he needed it.

By late August, he had transitioned from a wheelchair to crutches. The first time he took a step without support, the weight of it sent fire through his leg, but he bit down the scream, forcing his body to remember what it meant to move.

The room was quiet except for the faint buzz of a radio playing from the nurse's desk down the hall, some late-night public station or maybe a cassette on repeat. The voice was low, steady, philosophical in that post-hippie, pre-digital kind of way. His ears pricked up as the words drifted into the hall like a sermon for the broken.

"Have you ever wondered what the next 100 years would be like in 2100? We will all be buried with our relatives and friends.

Strangers will live in our homes, which we fought so hard to build. And then they will own everything we have today.

All our properties will be unknown. Including those things you spent fortune on, it will probably be scrapped. Our descendants will hardly know who we were, nor will they remember us. How many of us know our grandfather's father anyway?"

He closed his eyes, listening. For once, the voice didn't hurt. It didn't demand. It didn't sell. It just was. A small moment of grace. The voice on the radio continued

"After our death, we will be remembered for a few years. Then we will only be a portrait on someone's library. And a few years later our history, our photos, our deeds go into the dustbin of oblivion. History, we won't even be memories.

Maybe if one day we stop analyse these questions. We would understand how ignorant and weak the dream of obtaining everything was. If only we could think, certainly our approaches and our thoughts would change.

We would be like other people, always want to having more and more. And still feel like it's never enough, we took it for granted. Without having time for the things that are really worthwhile in this life.

We should change all that. To live and enjoy those walks we've never taken, those ungiven hugs, those kisses to our loves, those small talks we never had time for. Those would definitely be the best moments to remember.

At the end of the day, they would fill our lives with joy and happiness. And that is what we waste with greed and ignorance, day after day. But, there is still time for us, think about it. Do it from love, not for love.

Life is too short, stop worrying. It's okay, everything is supposed to be this way. You're supposed to feel this, it's all part of the process. This is part of it, take it and absorb it. Nothing lasts forever, it hurts, but it may be the only way.

Life is supposed to be a journey, is it not?"

That was a thought provoking philosophical thought by Bregas Maulana, Up next a little Deep Purple to help cement the thought…

The road ahead was long, but he was walking it, one painful step at a time. And then, the words returned. He hadn't thought about writing, not really. The act of survival had consumed him, leaving no room for anything else. But one morning, sitting at the makeshift desk his wife had arranged in the back room, he stared at the blank page and felt something stir inside him.

The first few sentences came slowly, clumsy and unsure like a man learning to walk again. But they came. Writing may not have saved his life, but it did what it had always done: it made his life a brighter, more pleasant place. The weeks pulled into months, each one marked by the slow, tedious march of rehabilitation. Every step on the crutches was a battle, every breath a reminder of what had been taken from him. His body was in ruin, held together with metal rods and surgical precision, but it was his mind that felt the most broken. Lost. The first time he sat at his desk again, it felt foreign beneath his hands. The pain of sitting longer than forty-five minutes was hideously unbearable; standing was unbearable. Nothing he could do alleviated the pain, the agony that wouldn't stretch out no matter how much the therapist tried, and boy, they tried.

The paper, once an extension of himself, was now just dead white space. The words had left him. Moloch had left him.

But muscle memory is a strange thing. Writing had been a ritual, a practice, a repetition of patterns drilled into him over decades. Even now, after everything, he could still feel the rhythm of keystrokes, the way sentences should move, the way a paragraph should breathe. He knew structure. He knew tone. He knew fear. He still knew how to write. Yet something had changed. The absence of Moloch had not just left him feeling empty, nor had it given him relief, it had left him altered, irrevocably shaped by something that had once burrowed into the deepest recesses of his mind. He had not merely been possessed; he had been rewritten, synapses formed that can't be torn apart and his thoughts stretched around an influence that refused to fully let go. The ink that once bled from him had not faded; it had thickened and curdled beneath his skin, staining the very marrow of his bones with something lingering, something patient.

The milk absorbs the flavour of whatever's next to it in the fridge as his mother used to say. A stray thought, insignificant, meaningless, yet it lingered in his mind longer than it should have. If something as simple as milk could take on the essence of whatever surrounded it; if it could be changed by mere proximity, then why not a man? Why not his words? How could he expect to be untouched by something that had lived within him for so long? Moloch was gone, but something of him remained, absorbed into the fabric of the writer's being, seeping into the spaces between his thoughts.

The writing space that Martha created for him to help him fill his days with something productive was all too familiar. He couldn't help but reminisce that the space seems to reflect the old writing nook he once had in the old trailer. He bought that old thing a few years back and burnt it to the ground in a drunken frenzy.

He pulled his wheelchair up to the desk and looked at the computer, then sees a yellow legal pad and decides that he's going old school. He wanted to write something new, something harmless. A recollection of the accident, the slow, agonising crawl of recovery, the monotonous rituals of physical therapy, the unyielding cycle of pain, pills, and waiting. It was an exercise in remembering more than anything, an attempt to make sense of the suffering, to put it down in a way that felt tangible. He always did that, wrote down his fears to help overcome them. But as he read over his own words, in his own handwriting something felt wrong. The tone was sharp, alive, unnatural even. It carried a level of urgency he hadn't intended, a pulsing narrative that he couldn't account for, like something beneath the ink was pressing it forward, waiting. And then, at the very bottom of the page, nestled between the last two lines he was certain he had written, was a sentence that he knows had not come from him.

YOU STILL REMEMBER, DON'T YOU?

Panic hit as hard as the car did, his skin tightening as his gaze fixed on the words. The ink was dry. It was his handwriting.

The question was real. His hands trembled as he stared, his pulse a hammering presence in his throat. The room was silent. The desk beneath his fingertips felt suddenly foreign, the air in the room pressing down against his skin. Looking up to rest his tired eyes he turned back to the page, eyes searching, scanning, nothing. The sentence was gone. The page was as it had been before, blank except for the words he had knowingly placed there. He squeezed his eyes shut, exhaling through clenched teeth, willing his heartbeat to slow. It was exhaustion, that's all. A lapse in focus. A trick of a fatigued mind. That's what he told himself as he shut the notebook, pushed away from the desk, and reached for his crutches with unsteady hands.

Milk absorbs flavour. Moloch may have been gone. But he had left his mark.

Even if Moloch was gone.

For nearly thirty years, the silence had remained unbroken. A ghost. A whisper lost in the void. Life had continued, he wrote another 30 titles, most of which turned into movies, Life had essentially unchanged in the ways that mattered most, and though the author had aged, though his body bore the scars of what had come before, the world had moved forward, indifferent to the ruin he carried within him. The stories came and went, books were published, interviews were conducted, and accolades were gathered, yet none of them ever felt quite the same. The fire that had once consumed him that had driven him to the edge of madness in pursuit of something greater had been reduced to embers, flickering at the periphery of his mind, threatening to go out completely. He was content, or at least as close to contentment as a man like him could ever be. The spectres of the past had faded into something distant, something buried.

Until one night on the other side of the world in a little town where his little bookshop had been his retreat, his sanctuary, a place where stories were contained, controlled, bound within the safety of their pages. Here, he was untouchable. Here, the past could not reach him, the future unknown. The glow of a single lamp flickered against the shelves, its feeble light casting long, slanted shadows that swayed with the movement of the air. Outside, the world was still, the inhabitants now settling in for the night, the kind of stillness that carried weight, that made the skin prickle on a cold night, as if something unseen had settled just beyond the edges of perception. Dust hung in the air, suspended in the quiet glow, coating the spines of long forgotten books, filling the empty spaces with something both hollow and wanting.

He leaned back in his chair, fingers drumming absently against the worn cover of an unfinished manuscript, his gaze unfocused, thoughts adrift in the steady rhythm of solitude. Thinking back to a conversation with a customer earlier that day. A budding author who dreamed of winning a *Booker* prize or hitting the coveted *New York Times* best sellers list, he remembers saying to him that if he ever wrote a book, he would rather get on the Pope's Do Not Read list the *Index Librorum Prohibitorum*. The budding author, confused, asked, 'Why?' The bookshop owner replied, '…cause then a billion Catholics would want to know why.' A grin took over his face as he thought back on that conversation, holding his unfinished manuscript dreaming of stardom.

And then, A presence.

Not a sound. Just an awareness. Pulling at the edges of his thought, like the sensation of being watched in an empty room. A shadow stretched long and dark oozing out of the bookshelves, its form shifting subtly, unnaturally, as if the very fabric of the dim light could no longer hold its shape. He stiffened, breath catching in his throat, fingers tightening around the armrests of his chair. He did not turn. He did not move. He didn't dare look. He only listened. Then a voice. Smooth. Deep. Seemingly familiar.

"Hello, Ian... a long pause... I've been waiting for you."
Another pause. A silence that was not empty but filled with knowing.
A smile unseen.
"My name is Moloch. If you'll indulge me, I have a story to share."

THE END

Acknowledgements

Let's get the formalities out of the way first, so we can descend into the chaos with clarity. This book was written in pieces, across time zones, mental states, and at least three different existential crises. If you're reading this, it means the manuscript survived, which, if you know anything about my habits, is a small miracle. But no creation happens alone, even if it's created in solitude and stitched together with coffee and anxiety.

So let's begin with the people who made sure I didn't abandon this thing in a fireproof safe marked DO NOT OPEN.

Martin, my quiet storm. My compass with an esoteric grin. If I ever accidentally start a cult, you're the first person I'm blaming. Your endless encouragement, maddening patience, and spiritual nudges kept me pointed vaguely forward. You know more than most there were times I wanted to throw in the towel, and you'd sit there, tilt your head, and remind me that the grave is permanent, problems are temporary.

Libbie. Where do I start? You've seen me at my worst. Not the forgot to shower worst, the there's nothing left in the tank and I'm not sure I care worst. And yet, you stayed my friend. You kept encouraging, kept reminding me I had something to say, even when I was mumbling it through clenched fists. You supported me through some things I wouldn't wish on anyone, and you never flinched. This book is glued with your support, line by line. It wouldn't exist without you.

Oscar, Mark, from one side of the planet to the other, you're the best mate I've ever known. You show up when most people evaporate. You listen without fixing. You joke without cruelty. And somehow, you make space in the world for people like me, even when I'm doing my level best to break it all. This book carries your fingerprint, even if you can't see it. The world doesn't deserve you. I barely do. But I'm grateful you're in my life, ya crazy pirate.

Kim. This is on you. You're the one who told me to write in the first place. I was content grumbling at walls and making enemies of inanimate objects. But you poked something in me, way back then, and it stuck. You saw a story before there was one. Whatever this thing has become, however twisted, broken, or beautiful, it started because you believed I could shape it. Thank you for lighting that particular fuse.

To my brothers in the craft, thank you for standing behind me even when I didn't know which direction I was facing. You've given me structure when my world had none, and a quiet sense of accountability I desperately needed. The square and compasses remind me to square my actions and circle back when I screw up, which is often. You've never let me fall without offering a hand, and for that, I am deeply grateful.

Now to my Patreon crew. The lifeblood. The ones who believed in me with their wallets, which, let's be honest, is the modern measure of belief. You didn't just say nice things. You funded the madness. Month after month, while I spun words into being and shaped shadows into stories, you kept showing up. That matters. That matters more than you probably know.

All of you are amazing, but especially these superhumans: Libbie (yes, again), Tina, Jean, Helen, Niche, James, Elsie, Sharon, Liz, Carol, Bobby, and Russell. You've carried this project more than you know. Your names made it into the pages. All of your support made it onto the page. You didn't just back the work, you backed me. And that's not something I'll ever forget.

To the rest of my Patreon members, thank you deeply. These legends happen to be on a higher tier, but not higher in my gratitude. Not even close.

There were moments I stared at the screen and saw nothing but static. Days where I wasn't sure if this story would survive the week, let alone be read by anyone else. What pulled me back, again and again, was knowing you were out there, waiting. Expecting. Hoping. You gave this thing weight when I felt weightless.

This book carries pieces of all the people who helped build it. I borrowed your names, but I never borrowed your souls. That would be Moloch's job.

There's no tidy way to end acknowledgements like these, because gratitude never really finishes. But if this book reaches anyone, really reaches them, it'll be because you were there behind the scenes, lending me your faith when mine was running on fumes.

This was never about fame. Never about money. It was an exorcism. About survival. About bleeding my heart onto the page because silence wasn't working. And some of you didn't just stand by me through that, you stood in front. Took the hit. Held the line.

Thank you.

About the Author

Do you really care?

Ian Bayly grew up in a boys' home in western Sydney, Australia, and got up to all sorts of mischief. What were they going to do, put him in a boys' home?

That same instinct, to push back, to question, to test the edges, never left him. He's travelled solo around the world, seen things most people only read about, and carries more emotional scars than he'd care to admit. He's owned a rare bookshop. He's won and lost a dozen small fortunes. He's been beaten down by life hard enough to stay down, but didn't. Turns out he's tougher than he looks. A bloody cockroach, I tell ya. Keeps crawling back. Keeps writing.

Experience taught him that pain has shape, silence has weight, and solitude, when chosen, is its own kind of power. The world never gave him a soft place to land, so he built one out of stories, sharp-edged, unclean, and unsettling as hell.

He writes fiction soaked in blood, grief, and rot, then wires it to a live current and calls it a story. His work doesn't nod politely to ancient truths. It drags them out by the roots, blinking into the light, teeth still wet. He doesn't write to entertain. He writes to excavate. And sometimes, what's buried doesn't stay quiet.

Moloch is his second novel in the Dark Matter mythos. It picks at the raw seam between addiction and possession, suffering and salvation, ambition and annihilation. If Dark Matter cracked open the void, Moloch steps in barefoot.

He doesn't believe in tidy endings, easy villains, or the kind of fiction that flatters the reader. His stories don't care if you're comfortable. They care if you're awake.

He wrote most of his next book, 86400 (still in editing), not in a single pub, but across dozens of them, from Penzance in the south of England to Thurso at the very top of Scotland, with about fifty questionable stops in between. Too many pints. Too many scribbled notes. Chasing down the right words between last call and the publican's glare. That's where he thinks best, half-distracted, full of questions, a little drunk, and nowhere else he'd rather be.

Ian now splits his time between wherever he's needed and wherever he can be left alone. He still walks alone. Still listens to the wrong voices. Still believes fiction is the last honest way to tell the truth.

If you've read this far, maybe you've already crossed the threshold.

Just keep going.

Connect with Ian
www.ianbayly.com
Facebook & Instagram: @ianbayly.author
Patreon.com/ianbayly

ASHLAR
PRESS

About Ashlar Press

Ashlar Press is an independent publisher dedicated to fiction that reflects imagination, discipline, and craft. The press was created to give writers a professional home where their stories are treated with dignity and presented to the highest standard.

We believe fiction is one of the most powerful ways to explore truth. A well-told story can illuminate the human experience, bridge cultures, and endure beyond its time. Our catalogue embraces every genre including romance, thriller, historical drama, speculative fiction and horror. What unites them is not subject matter but the integrity of the voices behind them.

Ashlar Press operates on two principles: integrity and empowerment. Every manuscript is handled with care and respect, and authors retain one hundred per cent of their rights and royalties. In this way, we ensure that each book remains the true work of its creator while reaching readers across the world through professional editing, design and distribution.

At Ashlar, we see each book as a carefully shaped stone, placed within a greater edifice of human creativity. Together they form a library built on imagination, reflection and the search for meaning.

For more information, visit ashlarpress.com

Boo!